The end h

Fourteen-year-old Vincent Drear's religion has taught him a couple of things. First, the world is going to end. Second, until it does, he has two jobs: saving souls and protesting movies about boy wizards. Vincent suspects there might actually be more to life and his suspicions are confirmed when he finds an elf at h

Unfortunately, the elf informs Vinc

religion is right about one thing: th

coming—in forty-eight hours!

Vincent would like to save the

stacles stand in his way—hungry der

elves, multinational corporations,

His only hope is to get his family

demons wipe out everything, pavin

epoch.

But the fun has just b

EPOCH

TIMOTHY CARTER

flux™
Woodbury, Minnesota

First Edition
First Printing, 2007

Book design by Steffani Sawyer
Book editing by Rhiannon Ross
Cover design by Lisa Novak
Cover illustration by Ken Wong

Flux, an imprint of Llewellyn Publications

Library of Congress Cataloging-in-Publication Data
Carter, Timothy, 1972–
  Epoch / Timothy Carter.—1st ed.
    p. cm.
  Summary: As the end of the world approaches, fourteen-year-old Vincent breaks away from his parents' religion and forms an odd alliance with a few other humans who have the ability to see the elves, pixies, and demons that are engaged in a battle to bring about a new epoch.
  ISBN-13: 978-0-7387-1066-2
  [1. End of the world--Fiction. 2. Supernatural--Fiction. 3. Religion--Fiction. 4. Science fiction.] I. Title.
  PZ7.C24825Ep 2007 [Fic]--dc22

                                                    2007009792

Flux
Llewellyn Publications
A Division of Llewellyn Worldwide, Ltd.
2143 Wooddale Drive, Dept. 978-0-7387-1066-2
Woodbury, MN 55125-2989, U.S.A.
www.fluxnow.com

Printed in the United States of America

Other Books by Timothy Carter

Attack of the Intergalactic Soul Hunters

Closets

Section K

Introduction

This is a story about the end of the world. It is not about some hero stopping it from ending, either. There are heroes in this story, and there are villains. There are fantasy creatures and magic users. There are battles, there are defeats, and there are victories.

But make no mistake, this is about the end of the world as we know it. There will be no calling off of the end at the last minute, no reprieve, no gosh-that-was-a-close-call sighs of relief.

This is it. The end has come.

But the fun has just begun. With that in mind, let us meet Vincent.

"The rogue planet will come," said the tall girl in the white turtleneck. "And when it does, it will destroy us all!"

The girl stood behind a table, upon which was a basketball painted to look like an alien world. Next to it stood a globe, with several natural disasters drawn in magic marker all over its surface.

Behind her on the wall was a large piece of bristol board, upon which was a detailed drawing of the alien planet's orbit. Above the drawing, in big red letters, were the words, "Rogue Planet."

Her name was Sandra. She was not Vincent.

"They already have agents in the White House and the Pentagon," said a Japanese boy in a T-shirt that featured a giant, gun-toting robot. "And soon, when the bulk of their fleet arrives in orbit, they'll take us down in seconds!"

On the table in front of him, he had displayed several alien action figures and a few plastic UFOs. He'd also placed pieces of human action figures around the display, just for effect. On the wall behind him were several imaginatively drawn pictures of aliens wiping out humanity.

His name was Pat. He was not Vincent, either.

"The world will end in ice!" said a thin Indian boy. "Weather patterns will change, and a new ice age will consume the planet."

He stood before a table littered with drawings of dangerous weather, with explanations written in note form. On the wall behind him, his bristol board poster read "The Next Ice Age" in blue lettering.

His name was Vijay. He also was not Vincent.

In fact, most of the kids presenting their projects at Woodlaw Middle School's 10th annual science fair were not Vincent. There were two Michaels, four Johns, and quite a few Jennifers, but only one of them was Vincent.

Vincent Drear stood behind his display in the far corner of the school's gymnasium, right next to the big orange drink dispenser. He wore a faded, worn pair of jeans, the same pair his mother had tried to throw out twice before. His sneakers were old and grubby, not the polished dress shoes his parents had wanted him to wear, and his T-shirt was loose and baggy. His clothes did not look very spectacular, but they were comfortable. Vincent liked comfortable clothes. They helped him to deal with situations he found uncomfortable, like the snickers he got when people saw his display.

On the table in front of Vincent, he had many leaflets and tracts from his parents' church. He also had small statues of Jesus Christ, Moses, and Abraham, the Holy Triumvirate. Vincent had placed them around a small globe, next to a stand-up sign that read, "The Act of Cleansing."

While the other students stood and shouted out their prophecies of doom, Vincent slouched in his chair and hoped he wouldn't be noticed.

"You're hoping nobody will notice you, right?" said Big Tom, the smallest person in the entire school. He wore a white shirt buttoned right up to his neck, and red corduroy pants that were hideous to look at. Big Tom sat on a couple of textbooks on top of a stool, and even then he could barely see over his table.

"You know the judges will be here eventually," Big Tom told his friend.

Vincent nodded but said nothing. His eyes were fixed on his older brother Max, who handed out leaflets from Vincent's table to anyone who would take one. Max was a large boy, dressed sharply in a red shirt and tie. His hair was immaculately cut and combed, and his blue eyes could only be described as piercing.

As Max stuffed pamphlets into hands, he preached for all he was worth, determined to save at least one soul at the science fair.

Vincent's family were Triumvirites, a new branch of Christianity that had popped up fairly recently on the spiritual marketplace. Triumvirites believed that three characters from the Bible—Jesus, Moses, and

Abraham—had banded together to produce a text that spelled out the definitive version of God's divine plan for the universe.

That text was the *Book of the Triumvirate*, discovered thirty years ago inside a cave outside Jerusalem. It spoke of dire times ahead, when demons would roam the earth spreading lies and deception. Only the Triumvirate could show people the true path, and save them from an eternity in fire.

Vincent hadn't asked for—or wanted—his brother's help. And he really hadn't wanted to do a display for his family's religion. He thought the whole Triumvirate thing was bunk, though he was smart enough to keep those feelings to himself.

Vincent turned his head and looked at the volcano display on Big Tom's table. The two friends had spent a week making it out of papier-mâché, and to Vincent's eye it looked great. Of course, he'd been the one who'd painted it. It was gray, the universal color of plain old rock, with red lava streaks and brown for trees from the mid-point on down. The cone at the top was ten centimeters wide, and filled with baking soda. On the table beside the volcano was a bottle of vinegar, which would react with the baking soda to produce a volcanic effect.

On the wall behind Big Tom was a sign that read "Volcanic Calamity." Vincent had come up with the title, which to his ear sounded much better than "Volcanoes Will End The World Someday With Their Thick Ash."

In Vincent's opinion, volcanoes were not going to wipe out the world. They could change the weather, sure—he remembered the extra-long winter they'd had a few years back when a volcano in Peru dumped three mountains worth of ash into the atmosphere. However, the idea that a volcano could put enough ash into the sky to end all life across the planet wasn't very likely.

A volcanic apocalypse was more likely, however, than the Holy Triumvirate coming down from the sky and announcing the end. Unfortunately for Vincent, that was exactly what he was supposed to be saying.

"Don't you think it's weird," Big Tom said suddenly, "that everyone's doing end-of-the-world stuff this year?"

"That's what the school decided the theme should be," Vincent said, his eyes fixed once more on his brother. "We had to do what they said."

"Well, yeah," Big Tom said. "But don't you think

it's weird they chose that as a theme? I mean, that's kind of morbid."

Vincent nodded. He didn't think it was weird at all, however. The school was simply going along with the latest fad.

Everyone was talking about the end-times these days. It seemed to have come from nowhere, as most fads did, but after two years it had achieved a kind of permanence. Not a week went by without the discovery of some new asteroid that might hit us, or a new terrorist group that might have the Bomb appearing on the world scene. Weathermen pointed to strange weather patterns and declared them the onset of something far more sinister.

And then, there were the religious cults. None of them called themselves cults, of course. They preferred the term "The One True Faith." Every day, it seemed, a One True Faith member got his or her name in the paper by leading some kind of march, rally, or protest. Sometimes they assembled outside a doctor's office, or the home of a politician who was pro-choice. Often they would rally at a bookstore, movie theater, or anywhere else where sinful deeds or images were on display.

And of course, all the cults preached that the end

of the world was nigh. However, none preached that message more enthusiastically than the Triumvirites. Vincent's family had dragged him to three End-Of-Day rallies since the start of the school term, and he hadn't enjoyed them at all.

Vincent hadn't had to do much work for his project—all the pamphlets and posters he used had been lying around the house. For that, and that alone, Vincent was glad of his family's religion. With everyone at home willing to prepare his project for him, he'd had plenty of time to help out Big Tom with his volcano.

"Vincent, the judges are coming!" Big Tom hissed. "What do I do?"

Vincent rolled his eyes. A good friend Tom most certainly was. A smart boy he most certainly was not.

"Use the notes I gave you when they ask questions," Vincent said, tapping one of the papers on Big Tom's table. "Then, when they want a demonstration, pour some vinegar on the baking soda."

"I remember that part," Big Tom said, grabbing the bottle of vinegar. "It's just…you'll help me out, won't you?"

"You bet," Vincent said. "Just relax. It's only a science fair."

"Yeah," Big Tom said, "but I want to win!"

"You won't," Vincent said. "And neither will I. Barnaby Wilkins will win. He always does."

Big Tom had nothing to say to that. They both looked over at the table in the center of the gymnasium, which stood before a big billboard poster that read, "Government Conspiracy" in big red letters. Behind that table stood a tall, wiry boy, dressed in khakis, a collared shirt, and a V-necked sweater. He did not fit the typical image of the school bully, but Vincent and Big Tom knew only too well that his outward appearance was deceiving.

On the table in front of Barnaby, two laptops ran a slide show of images, complete with sound effects and narration from two large speakers on either side. The thumping musical accompaniment was, in Vincent's opinion, a bit much.

But that wasn't the best of it. Barnaby's two bodyguards, Bruno and Boots, stood on either side of Barnaby, glaring at passersby. Dressed in black suits and dark glasses, they waved official-looking badges and snapped dialogue like, "That's classified information!" or "You've seen too much!" at anyone who cared to listen.

"You've got to admit," Vincent sighed, "he knows how to put on a show."

Barnaby's father, Francis Wilkins, was rich. He was not Let's-Buy-the-Statue-of-Liberty-for-Barnaby's-Birthday kind of rich, but he had more than enough and a bit more besides. He was a top executive at Alphega Corp., one of the largest and most profitable corporations in the world, and his position paid very, very well. Every year he spared no expense to make sure his son's projects were the best they could be. It made all the other kids jealous, and it always made the judges swoon.

"Well, what have we here?" said one of the judges as they arrived at Big Tom's table. He was short, sweaty, and bald, and smelled vaguely of cheese.

"This is…well, my project is on volcanoes," Big Tom said.

"Is that what this is supposed to be?" said another judge, tapping the volcano's side. "I thought it was a smokestack or something." He was tall, thin, and balding, with glasses so thick they made his eyes comically huge.

"It's a volcano," Vincent said, glaring at the thoughtless adults who had dared to put down his creation.

"We'll be right with you, son," the cheesy judge said.

"So," the third judge asked Tom, "you think volcanoes are going to take over the world, eh?" She was pear-shaped, with a tiny chest above her huge thighs and enormous bottom. She had way too much makeup on her face, and her long and spindly fingers resembled spider legs.

"Um, er…well, yes! That's my project," Big Tom said, looking frantically at Vincent for help.

Vincent sighed, then mimed with his hands the idea of volcanoes erupting and spewing out so much ash into the atmosphere that the sun would be blocked and the planet would freeze. He really did. You can mime anything with your hands if you try.

"Um…so, all these volcanoes will erupt," Big Tom said, "and cover the entire planet in ash…"

Vincent put his hands in his face and moaned.

"You should be concerned with your own project, brother."

Vincent looked up and saw Max standing in front of his table, staring pure disapproval into his face. Vincent sighed again; he'd only taken his eyes off his brother for thirty seconds, a minute at most.

"Why are you not preaching the Good Word?" Max went on, perfectly pronouncing the capital letters on Good and Word. "I'm out there distributing pamphlets for you, spreading the Message of the Triumvirate, and you sit and do nothing."

"I'm pacing myself," Vincent said. "I want to save my energy for when it really matters."

"It always matters!" Max snapped. "Every moment of life must be spent spreading the Joyous Love of the Triumvirate."

Whereas Vincent had more or less given up the faith, Max had embraced it wholeheartedly. For a while Vincent thought his brother's belief was just a way of sucking up to their parents. And maybe that had been Max's intention in the beginning. Now, however, it was clear to Vincent his brother was a True Believer.

Max often said the Triumvirate gave his life Direction and Meaning. Vincent thought it made his brother a major pain in the rear. Especially when that Direction and Meaning were shoveled into Vincent's face.

"Why don't you go save someone?" Vincent suggested.

"You mean Save?"

"Yeah, that."

"I want to see how well you do with the judges," Max said. "If they are not impressed, Mother and Father will be most unhappy."

Vincent made a face at his brother, then returned his attention to Big Tom's vain attempt to please the judges. He was trying to pour some vinegar into the volcano to set off the baking soda, but he couldn't quite reach the top and vinegar was slopping all over the side.

Vincent moaned, then got up and took the vinegar from his friend. He poured it into the volcano's cone, and absolutely nothing happened.

"Well, that's not very good," the bug-eyed judge said.

"That should have worked," Vincent said, confused. "Big Tom, more baking soda."

Big Tom grabbed his half-full bag of baking powder and tried to spoon some more in. As he did so, Vincent got a good look at the bag and made an unpleasant discovery.

"This," he snatched the bag away from his friend, "is flour."

"It is?" Big Tom said. "It looked the same as baking soda, so I just figured it was the same thing."

"It is not," Vincent said, "the same thing. I told you so many times…"

"Did you help him with this project?" the spider-finger judge asked.

"That's against the rules," said bug-eyes.

"I'm afraid you two will have to be disqualified," said the cheesy judge, making a mark on his clipboard.

"But...but..." Big Tom said, but the judges were already walking away.

"Don't you want to see mine?" Vincent called after them.

"Why bother?" the cheesy judge called back. "You're disqualified."

Vincent sat down heavily and glared at Big Tom. Max leaned down on his table and glared at him.

"Mother and Father will be very disappointed," Max said.

"Oh, go away," Vincent replied, standing back up and shoving some more pamphlets into his brother's hands.

"Very disappointed," Max repeated, in case the first time hadn't sunk in. When Vincent didn't respond, Max assumed it had.

However, it hadn't. At that moment, Vincent saw something a lot more interesting under one of the other tables. It was smaller than Big Tom, brown-skinned and pointy-eared, and it wore clothing that seemed to have been fashioned from leaves. Vincent thought for a moment that it was a toy or something, but then it turned its head and its big, deep eyes locked with his. Its big eyes grew wider, possibly in surprise, and then it seemed to grin.

Max turned and left. The movement distracted Vincent, and he lost sight of the creature. When he looked under the table again, it was gone.

"What," he asked no one, "was that?"

"I don't know," Big Tom said, thinking Vincent was talking to him.

Vincent could have said something silly, like, "Did you just see that?" but it was clear that Big Tom had not. Vincent sat back down, and stared at the spot where the thing had been. A shiver went through him. There was only one thing he could think of that the creature might have been. Something his parents, brother, and priest had warned him about all of his life.

A demon.

Only last Sunday, he'd been subjected to a sermon on demons.

"They are everywhere," Pastor Impwell had preached to their congregation of forty-two people. "They seek to do harm to our souls, lead us away from the Truth, and into a Web of Sin. That is why we must be ever Vigilant. Listen not to those who would accuse you of paranoia or fear mongering, my friends. Demons are real, and we must educate the world of their existence."

The sermon had bored Vincent to tears at the time, but now it didn't seem quite so stupid. That creature he'd seen might have been a demon, a possibility that held terrible implications. If demons were real, did that also mean the Triumvirate was real as well?

Because if they were, he was in some major spiritual trouble.

The drive home was torture, but Vincent had expected no less. His parents had listened very carefully while Max gave his report of Vincent's shortcomings, then they expressed their own grave disappointment.

"You'd better have a good explanation for not

preaching the Message with all your Strength," his father said.

"Indeed," added Max, who didn't want to be left out.

Vincent had heard it all before. "You're letting the Triumvirate down, Vincent." "I don't know what Pastor Impwell will say, Vincent." "Don't you feel the Fire in your soul, Vincent?" "You know how important the Message is, Vincent!"

Vincent said, "Yes, Mom," and "Yes, Dad," when expected, responding on autopilot. His mind, however, was on greater issues.

He'd seen a demon. That, at least, was what he feared the creature to be. He'd considered telling his brother about it, but Max would have thought he was making it up to get himself out of trouble.

Of course, if Max had seen it, he would have declared it a demon immediately. There would have been no doubt at all in his mind. Vincent's mind was more open, and he hated to pass judgment without first knowing all the facts. He'd never seen a demon before, and didn't know what one was supposed to look like. That creature could have been anything.

But what if it was a demon? The thought terrified Vincent, but his open mind forced him to consider it.

He'd dismissed his family's religion as a stupid waste of time, but what if they'd been right on the money? What if demons really were trying to lead his soul away from the Triumvirate and into the fiery clutches of Hell?

To get his mind off his impending eternal damnation, Vincent gave his attention back to his parents.

"There will be no supper tonight for you, my son," said his mother. "For your own good. You've got to learn…Oh. It's that girl." Her voice, already harsh, had grown a shade darker.

Vincent had a look out the right side of the car and saw a teen girl sitting on the front lawn of a small bungalow. She had long, dark hair that had been dyed purple below her shoulders, and she wore a dress of the same color. She sat with her eyes closed on a small blanket, her hands turned upward in her lap.

"Chanteuse Sloam," Max said with distaste.

"What is she doing?" his mother wanted to know.

"Probably communing with evil spirits," their father replied knowledgeably.

"She's meditating," Vincent said, leaning to get a better look. He remembered she was pretty, but he'd forgotten how pretty.

Chanteuse had babysat Vincent and Max, back

when they were kids. Max hadn't liked her much, but Vincent took to her immediately. She'd played with him and told him about mystic energies, astral travel, and worlds beyond our own, and Vincent had sat listening to her for hours.

He missed those days.

"I don't care what that witch is doing," his mother said. "Why can't she do it somewhere else where we can't see her?"

"Maybe she likes the front lawn," Vincent said.

"You will go down to the chapel as soon as we get home," his father said. "You will pray for better Guidance, that you might preach the Message more competently in the future. Friday in particular."

"Yes, father," Vincent said, turning away from the Sloam house.

"Are we still going to the movie?" Max asked.

"Yes, dear," his mother replied. "As soon as we drop your brother off. Would you get the picket signs out of the garage?"

"Yes, Mother, I will," Max said, beaming a bright smile.

"You guys are actually protesting a movie tonight?" Vincent asked.

"If we get there quickly enough," his mother said.

It wasn't often that the Drear family, or indeed any Triumvirite, got to protest outside a movie theater or book launch or any other media-related event. They wanted to, but those opportunities were usually gobbled up by the other True-Faith groups. Such groups, being the One True Faith, refused to share when it came to their outrage, so the Triumvirites were often forced to picket other things.

Like acne. The sin they hide shall rise to the surface, the Book of the Triumvirate said, so Triumvirites often staked out drug stores. Exercise gyms were another no-no, for attempting to change one's body was to reject the form God had given you. Protests at such locations caused little more than quizzical glances, but for Triumvirites it was the thought, and the effort, that counted.

Tonight, however, the local Triumvirite congregation had a chance to picket an actual, honest-to-gosh motion picture. Assuming, of course, they beat the other One True Faiths to the cinema.

The Drear home was a large two-level house, made with red bricks. Max leapt out of the car the moment they arrived, and he ran to the garage and unlocked it. Inside were all their picket signs, ready for every occasion.

Max shuffled through the anti-acne signs and the say-no-to-the-devil's-gym sandwich boards until he found the ones for tonight's event. He chose the three best ones, and had them loaded into the trunk before Vincent and his father reached the front door.

"So what movie is it?" Vincent asked as they entered the house.

"It's the latest one with that boy wizard," his father replied as he steered him down the stairs.

"Ah," Vincent said. "You've got a good chance, then. The other groups gave up after part four."

"We could have used your help," his father went on, "but you clearly aren't in the Spirit. I just pray the Light finds you again in time for the event on Friday."

Vincent said nothing. He already had a plan in mind, and he didn't want his father to ruin it by not locking him in the chapel.

"Can I have a snack, at least?" he asked.

"No," his father said. "Fasting will do your spirit good."

"Won't do my tummy any good," Vincent muttered as his father shoved him inside.

"That's enough!" his father bellowed as he slammed

the two chapel doors together. "Start praying, and may the Triumvirate have mercy upon you."

The chapel was a small room with no windows, with an altar set up at the far end. The walls were bare and the floor was cold concrete, and the door had a thick padlock on the outside. Pastor Impwell had encouraged all in his congregation to construct one in their homes. They will be needed during the End Times, he'd said, when it will be too dangerous to venture out of doors even for Church. And until those End Times, they would serve as excellent discipline for wicked children.

Vincent knelt on the cold concrete floor and pretended to pray. His father snapped the padlock shut and stormed back upstairs.

Vincent waited until he heard the car tear off down the road. When he was sure they were gone, he escaped.

Vincent had learned a lot from his many hours locked in the chapel. He'd learned to entertain himself with his mind, and he'd learned to stop fearing the dark. He'd learned how to sleep on a hard surface, and he'd learned to rely on himself.

Most of all, he'd learned that while the padlock was nigh indestructible, the hinges holding up the doors were not. They were loose; one good upward shove would dislocate them from the wall.

Vincent grabbed one of the doors by its handle and bottom, then pushed up. He'd also learned he didn't need to pop both doors; when one was free, he could push the whole thing open like a regular door. Vincent lifted slowly, carefully, until the right hand door was free. Then he swung the door out, stepped out into the basement, and closed the door again.

Perfect. Now he had more than four hours to himself. There were an infinite number of things he could have done with the time, and on any other day he would have hung out at Big Tom's house.

Tonight, however, he needed to talk to someone about the creature he'd seen at the science fair. He could talk to Big Tom, but his friend would have no answers for him. He couldn't talk to his parents or brother, either. They would only confirm his fears. Besides, they were gone for the night.

That left one person. Vincent hurried up the stairs, grabbed his jacket, and left the house. Five minutes later, he reached the house of Chanteuse Sloam.

As he'd expected, Chanteuse was still meditating on her front lawn. He'd often seen her meditating on her front lawn when he passed her house going to and from school. People in cars would honk their horns and call her nasty things, and Vincent was always impressed how she never let it affect her. He'd never seen her lose concentration, and he'd only seen her upset once…

• • •

When he'd been ten, Chanteuse had told Vincent about performing simple magic spells, unaware that Max was listening. Max had rushed off to call their parents, who in turn rushed home and fired Chanteuse on the spot.

"How despicable!" his mother said. "Trying to teach my boys the ways of the Devil."

"You are a horrible creature, less than human," his father added. "You will suffer an eternity of torment for your sins."

"I'm sorry you feel that way," Chanteuse said, calm and pleasant. "I meant you and your family no harm…"

"Deceiver!" Mr. Drear shouted. "You mean nothing but harm for all of God's Children."

"I understand now," said Vincent's mother, "why your mother never shows herself in public."

"That isn't her mother," Mr. Drear said. "This girl was adopted. Probably abandoned on that horrible

Sloam woman's doorstep when your real parents discovered how evil you are."

Vincent felt the air around him change, as if it were getting thick and heavy. Chanteuse's face contorted into a visage of rage, and it was a terrifying thing to see.

"Miss Sloam is my mother," she said, "and you will never speak that way about her! Ever!"

"This is my house, I'll say what I like," Mr. Drear said, but he was visibly shaken. "Now get out of here and never come back."

Chanteuse left then, tears streaming from her eyes. Vincent would have protested, but a slap in the face from his brother stopped him.

"You should have known better," Max said.

"Your brother is right," his father agreed, taking Vincent's arm and yanking him down to the basement. "You will spend tonight in the chapel to contemplate your sin."

"For how long?" Vincent replied as he rubbed his cheek.

"Until you are cleansed of her evil," his father said as he shoved Vincent inside the chapel. "Kneel, and pray for cleansing and forgiveness."

"I don't understand!" Vincent protested. "What did she do?"

"She is a witch," his father said as he locked the door. "'Thou shalt not suffer a witch to live.' It's in the Text of the Triumvirate. So she is lucky I let her go. Kneel and pray, Vincent."

Vincent knelt on the cold concrete floor and began to pray. It was not the first time he'd been locked in there, nor would it be the last.

It was, however, the time that Vincent started asking himself some serious questions. What kind of a God, he'd wondered, would think Chanteuse was evil? If the Triumvirate preached Love, why did they insist their followers practiced so much hate? And if demons really are everywhere, spreading their lies and wickedness, why hasn't anyone ever seen one?

Vincent had prayed all night for answers to his questions, but none came. And the more he'd thought about the Triumvirate, the less any of it made sense. Vincent hadn't realized it then—realization would come in the weeks and months that followed—but his days of being a Triumvirite were over.

• • •

Vincent didn't want to disturb Chanteuse, so he sat on the ground in front of her and patiently waited. It had been a long time since he'd talked to her, not since the incident with his parents. Would she still be willing to talk to him?

"Hello, Vincent," Chanteuse said, her eyes still closed.

"Oh. Hi," Vincent replied, amazed but not really surprised. "How did you know it was me?"

"I sensed your energy," she said. "Everyone has a unique presence. I told you that."

"Yeah, I remember now," Vincent said. "Look, if you're not done…"

"I was just finishing," Chanteuse said, opening her eyes. They were emerald green, and Vincent could have sworn they glowed. "The Earth is restless, troubled. And so are you."

"I'm okay," Vincent said as she stood and picked up her rug. "But I need to talk to you about something."

"Come inside," she said. "We'll have tea and talk on the back porch."

Vincent followed her into the bungalow. It was a small home, with only two bedrooms, a living room, a kitchen and a tiny little basement. Chanteuse's adoptive mother, Miss Sloam, sat on the living room couch across from the front door, snoozing. Miss Sloam was a big woman; big boned, not fat.

Vincent had never been inside Chanteuse's house before, and he wondered briefly if she'd been embarrassed to have him over. His mother once told him that poor people were ashamed of their poverty. Vincent dismissed the thought straight away. He couldn't imagine Chanteuse being embarrassed about anything.

"Will you put the kettle on?" Chanteuse asked. "I need to get a fresh box of tea from the pantry in the basement."

"Sure, no problem," Vincent said. He filled up the kettle and plugged it in, then went in search of milk, sugar, and two cups. The milk was easy, right in the fridge where it should've been. The cups were in a cupboard, also an easy find.

The sugar was harder to find, and when Vincent did find it he lost interest in it immediately. He opened a cupboard and saw a bag of sugar on the first shelf, but his attention was immediately grabbed by the creature.

It was short and spindly, with almond-shaped eyes and big floppy wiener-dog ears. In fact, it looked exactly like the creature he'd seen at school.

And it was looking at him.

"Do you mind?" the thing said. "I'm trying to eat!"

Vincent stared at the creature in his former babysitter's cupboard, unsure of what to do. He'd come to talk about a creature like this, but here one was in the flesh. Was it a demon? Was it proof of the Triumvirate's existence? Vincent needed to know, but was too scared to ask.

"Got a staring problem, kid?" the thing said.

"Apparently, yes," Vincent replied. "Who, and what, are you?"

"I am a creature of Magic," the creature said, "who does not like to be disturbed. Flee before my dust of power!" And he threw a handful of sugar into Vincent's face.

"Ow!" Vincent said, staggering back and blinking the sugar out of his eyes.

The creature dropped to the floor, dashed between Vincent's legs and made for the back door. He almost made it when, like lightning, Chanteuse's hand lashed out and caught him by the ear.

"Ow!" the creature cried as he was lifted into the air. "Ow, ow, ow!"

"What have I told you about coming into the house?" she asked, holding the creature at eye level.

"What's going on in there?" Miss Sloam called from the living room.

"Just having a word with one of the wood people," Chanteuse replied.

"Another one?" her mom said. "We need an exterminator."

"What," Vincent asked, "is that thing?"

"I'm not a thing!" the creature said as he struggled in Chanteuse's grip. "I'm a magical being of power!"

"You look more like a shaved monkey," Vincent said.

"Stop, you two," Chanteuse said. "Ah, the kettle has boiled. Vincent, will you please make the tea and join me on the back porch?"

Chanteuse opened the back door and left before Vincent could ask anything else. Vincent took a moment to collect his thoughts and steady himself, then he prepared the tea. He had no doubt Chanteuse would fill him in when she was ready.

"Oh, thank you, Vincent," she said when he came out. He carried a tray loaded down with the teapot, milk, sugar, and two cups. "Grimbowl, please help my friend with the door."

"Hey!" said the creature as he held open the door for Vincent. "I see only two cups. Is someone going without?"

"Yeah, you," Vincent said, setting the tray down on the porch table. "That's what you get for throwing sugar in my face."

"I'll fetch you a cup in a moment," Chanteuse said, taking the pot and filling the two cups. "I want you to meet my friend Vincent. Vincent," she turned to him, "this is Grimbowl, an elf."

"An...elf?" Vincent asked, offering the tiny creature a wave. "Does he bite?"

"Do I bite?" the elf said, stung. "Do I bite? I look like a dog to you? I don't bite, kid, but I've been known to kick!" And he did, hard and strong into Vincent's left shin.

"Ow!" Vincent cried, clutching his leg and hopping. "You little jerk!"

"You want me to go for the other one?" Grimbowl asked.

"You want me to go for your head?" Vincent replied, rearing his left leg back.

"You two, stop," Chanteuse said. "Let's sit and have tea like peaceful beings."

Vincent put his leg down.

And Grimbowl kicked it again. Vincent collapsed into a chair, howling with pain, and the elf laughed. Then, faster than Vincent would have thought possible, Grimbowl leapt off the porch and sprinted away into the bushes at the back of the yard.

"I'm sorry about that," Chanteuse said, putting down her tea and checking Vincent's leg. "Elves are very mischievous creatures, but Grimbowl is usually better behaved."

"An elf," Vincent said. "That's a relief. I was worried he was something else."

"Did you think he was a demon?" Chanteuse asked with a smile.

"How did you know?" Vincent said, stunned.

"I've met your family, Vincent," Chanteuse said, handing him his tea. "I know the fears they must have put in your head. Everything strange or out of the ordinary must be something evil, am I right?"

"Pretty much," Vincent said. "But how do you know it isn't a demon? He could be deceiving you."

"Do you believe he's a demon?" Chanteuse asked. "Don't think. Just answer."

"No," Vincent said. "What you're telling me feels right. It's just...the Triumvirate warn that demons are everywhere, always trying to get us. I don't want to believe that, but what if it's..."

"Any organization that encourages you to fear," Chanteuse told him, "isn't worth following. Remember that, Vincent."

Vincent smiled. This was exactly what he'd been hoping for. He told Chanteuse about the elf he'd seen at the school science fair, and she listened without interrupting.

"I didn't know what it was," he finished, "so I came to ask you."

"I'm flattered you thought to come to me," she said, and Vincent blushed. Being around her just felt good.

"Elves usually avoid places where people gather," Chanteuse went on. "And Grimbowl never used to come inside the house until a couple of months ago. He and the others would only talk to me in the back-yard, and even then only because this house backs onto a park. In fact, when I first met the elves, they would only speak to me through the bushes."

"You know them pretty well," Vincent said.

"I only know what they tell me, which usually isn't much," Chanteuse told him. "Mostly they keep to them-selves."

"You know any other weird creatures?" Vincent asked.

"Only you, Vincent," she replied.

"You know what I mean!" Vincent cried, sloshing tea onto his pants. "Creatures like elves. Supernatural creatures like ghosts and goblins and fairies and man this tea is hot! Ow!"

"All creatures are part of the natural world, Vincent," she said. "Elves, ghosts, pixies, and others are as much a part it as you or I. For some reason, most people cannot perceive them. I think it is because they are unwilling."

"I can see them," Vincent said. "At least, I can see elves."

"Good for you," Chanteuse said. "Your mind is open, as I've always said. The world needs more people like you."

Vincent blushed again. "What about vampires?" he asked.

"Don't be silly," Chanteuse replied. "Vampires are make-believe."

They drank their tea and continued to chat. Vincent asked her to tell him more about elves, and she told him what she knew.

"Elves are like the first-nations peoples," she explained. "They live in harmony with nature. They live longer than humans do, in some cases for thousands of years."

"Are they magical?" Vincent wanted to know.

"Yes," Chanteuse said. "They use the energy fields that occur naturally on our planet to blend in with their surroundings, another reason so few people see them. I think if Grimbowl really hadn't wanted to be seen, you would not have seen him."

"Neat," Vincent said. "What else can they do? Fly? Move objects with their minds?"

"I truly don't know," Chanteuse said. "We'll ask the next time we see one.

"And now, Vincent, I must ask you to go. I have to get ready for work."

Vincent nodded, and together they cleaned up the tea. He felt worlds better for having talked to her. A strange feeling came over him; he knew something about the world that most people didn't. He doubted even the Holy Triumvirate had met and talked with elves.

Of course, they probably hadn't been kicked in the shin by one, either. Vincent wasn't sure if he'd made a friend or an enemy, but if Chanteuse liked Grimbowl then he was probably okay.

"Where are you working these days?" Vincent asked as Chanteuse put the teacups away. His parents had been more than thorough in spreading bad words about her, so it was unlikely she was still a babysitter.

"The grocery store at Dufferin and Steeles," Chanteuse replied. "I'm a cashier."

"You mean that Alphega Corp. Superstore?" Vincent asked.

"Yes, Vincent," Chanteuse sighed.

Vincent couldn't believe it. Chanteuse wasn't one to hate, but she really had it in for big corporations like Alphega. She'd told him about them once, back when she still babysat him. Vincent had asked if they could grab dinner at the nearby Steinburger's, and Chanteuse refused him on moral grounds.

"Steinburger's is owned and run by Alphega Corp.," she'd told him. "They are a very bad company, Vincent, and I will not support them."

"What's so bad about them?" Vincent had asked. He was still at the age where nothing tasted as good as a fried hamburger.

And so Chanteuse had told him. Told him about Alphega's reliance on sweatshops in China to produce its goods. Told him how Alphega Superstores would put local stores out of business. Told him how badly they treated their employees. Then she told him where the meat from a Steinburger's hamburger came from, and he threw up in the toilet.

"I guess they pollute the environment, too," Vincent had said as he wiped his mouth. Whenever Chanteuse talked about big corporations, usually it was because they were damaging Mother Earth.

"Actually, no," she'd said. "Their environmental

record is spotless. It's the one good thing I can say for them."

"So they're not all bad?"

"Not all bad," Chanteuse had admitted, "but certainly not good."

"I thought you were dead-set against those guys," Vincent said.

"I am," Chanteuse said, "but it was the only job I could find, and I need to support my mother."

"Right," Vincent said, making a mental note to keep his parents away from that superstore at all costs. "I just hope they don't treat you as badly as…hey, it's Big Tom."

And indeed it was. Chanteuse's house backed onto a park, and through that park went a bicycle path. Walking along that path, his head down and his pace sluggish, was Big Tom.

"He's upset," Chanteuse said. "His aura is dark blue."

"I'd better check on him," Vincent said. "May I leave through the back?"

"Certainly, Vincent," Chanteuse said, then smiled brightly. "Thank you for stopping by. It was wonderful to see you again."

Vincent felt himself blush again. He offered her an

awkward wave, then turned and ran through the bushes. A minute later, Vincent stood on the bike path beside his friend.

"Big Tom," he said, when his friend didn't immediately notice him. "What's wrong?"

"Huh? Oh, hi Vincent," Big Tom said, turning to look at him. When he did so, Vincent saw his friend had a fresh black eye.

"Woah! What happened?" he asked.

"What do you think?" Big Tom replied. "Barnaby Wilkins got me again."

"He did?" Vincent said. "Man, usually you're too fast for him."

It was true. What Big Tom lacked in size and strength, he made up for in speed. Bullies who wanted a piece of him had to catch him first, and for many this simply wasn't possible.

"One of his bodyguards held me down," Big Tom said.

"Oh," said Vincent, who'd had a brush himself with Barnaby Wilkins's two minders. "Which one was it? Bruno, or Boots?"

"Bruno," said Big Tom. "I hate him. He's the worst one."

Vincent could only nod in agreement. The school board wasn't exactly crazy about any student having two bodyguards with them at all times, but Mr. Wilkins had convinced them to see things his way. Alphega Corp. provided funding for the school and food for the cafeteria, so when an Alphega executive like Francis Wilkins wanted a favor for his son, the school board really couldn't say no.

And when a teacher saw those bodyguards holding students down for Barnaby to beat, all they could do was look the other way.

"Did Barnaby have a reason this time," Vincent asked, "or was it just a random beating?"

"He was gloating about winning the science fair," Big Tom said, "so I said he only won because his dad bought him all that high-tech stuff. That's when Bruno grabbed me."

"Are you hurt?" Vincent asked.

"He got me good in the face," Big Tom said, pointing to his black eye. "And he slugged me in the stomach, too."

"I'm sorry to hear that," Vincent said. "Why don't you come over to my place for a while? My family won't be back for a few hours, and I've got something really cool to tell you."

"You aren't telling him anything."

Vincent recognized the voice instantly. He spun around and looked down, and saw Grimbowl staring up at him.

"What is it?" Big Tom asked.

"Keep your mouth shut if you know what's good for you," Grimbowl told Vincent. "You're coming with us."

"Oh, am I?" Vincent said, assuming a defensive stance.

"Yes, you are," Grimbowl said, and Vincent suddenly realized they were surrounded by elves. There were about two dozen of them at least, blending in with the grass around them.

"What are you looking at?" Big Tom wanted to know.

"Them!" Vincent replied, gesturing all around him.

"What, the grass?" Big Tom said.

"No, you idiot!" Vincent said. "At the…ow!" He clutched at his shin and glared murder down at Grimbowl.

"Did you hurt yourself?" Big Tom asked. "What happened?"

And then Vincent understood. Chanteuse had said that few people could perceive elves. Big Tom simply couldn't see them.

"Your friend Vincent left," an older and wiser-looking elf said to Big Tom. "He has gone home. You should, too."

"I think I'll go home," Big Tom said, and he began to walk away.

"Big Tom!" Vincent cried, but his friend did not stop.

"No one can help you now," Grimbowl said. "Elves, take him."

While his best friend Big Tom walked away, blissfully unaware of what was going on, Vincent was set upon by elves. They swarmed all over him, their tiny hands grabbing and poking.

"Get off me!" Vincent yelled, pulling at them and trying to fling them off. He struggled hard, but there were too many elves and they pulled him down. So far they weren't using any weapons, but that didn't mean they wouldn't.

It seemed so unfair. Vincent had only just learned of a world beyond his own. Now it looked like he was going to die because of it.

Well, not without a fight! The elves were pulling him down, so Vincent went with it and threw himself forward. He landed smack-dab on a whole bunch of surprised elves, knocking them all flat. The tiny little "oof" noises were music to Vincent's ears.

The elves recovered quickly, however. Vincent had forgotten their speed; in no time they tied his legs together and pinned him down on the ground. Vincent rolled himself over, dislodging a few elves and steamrolling a few others, but all too soon he was overwhelmed. The strength in their little arms was incredible, and their numbers too many. Seconds later, Vincent's hands were tied as well. He was helpless, and at the elves' mercy.

"You are helpless and at our mercy," the wise-looking elf said, "so cease your struggles."

"Let's chop him into bits!" said an elf whom Vincent had rolled over.

"Yeah," agreed another as he helped his friend back up. "Then we'll feed those bits to the birds."

"You will not!" Vincent said, struggling for all he was worth. The ropes felt like dandelion leaves, but they were really strong.

"I said," the wise elf said as he reached into his robe, "stop doing that." He produced a little bag, and from there he pulled out a handful of dust.

"We're bringing him to the chief," Grimbowl said as the wise elf blew the dust into Vincent's face. "This kid might actually be the one we've been looking for."

If they said anything more, Vincent didn't hear it. The moment the dust touched his face, he fell sound asleep.

● ● ●

When Vincent awoke, his head felt very heavy. He realized after a moment or two that he was hanging upside down. He snapped his eyes open, and saw a whole lot of tree.

"What the…" he said, twisting himself around to get a better look at his surroundings. He couldn't see much, what with the lack of light, but he could just make out that he was hanging from a tree branch. He heard voices coming from above him, but they were too faint for him to make them out.

"This isn't good," Vincent said, and gave his ropes a quick struggle. Nope, they were just as strong as before. He felt around for the knots, hoping to untie himself, but his fingers found none. If there was only some more light, he thought, then I might be able to see some way to escape.

And then it hit him. It was dark because it was nighttime. He'd been out for so long that the sun had gone down. He had no way of knowing what the time was, which only made things worse. If he didn't get home before his parents and brother, whatever these elves had planned for him would be a picnic compared with what they'd do.

"Help!" Vincent cried. "Somebody help me!"

"Well, look who's awake."

It was Grimbowl's voice, but Vincent couldn't see him.

"Help!" Vincent screamed. "I'm up in a tree, and…ow!" His jaw stung from what had felt like a kick.

"Stop that," Grimbowl said. "You're wasting your breath, anyway. Nobody can hear you up in this tree."

"They can't?" Vincent said.

"All the leaves of this tree are affected by our magic," Grimbowl said, and Vincent could just make out the elf's arm gesturing expansively at the branches. "It's kind of like the dust Optar threw in your face. That stuff was set to make you sleep, just as the leaves are set to keep in sound."

"I see. Interesting," Vincent said. And inconvenient for me, he thought. "How long have I been hanging here?"

"About three hours," Grimbowl told him.

"Three hours?" Vincent barked. "Let me down from here right now!" He renewed his struggling, panic overriding common sense.

"Stop that," Grimbowl said, kicking Vincent's face again. "You'll never break free. The grass we made the ropes from are set to not break."

"Stop kicking me," Vincent said, his body swinging back and forth from the blow. "I have to get home, or I'll be in deep trouble."

"You're already in deep trouble," Grimbowl pointed out.

"Not as deep as I will be," Vincent said.

"Aren't you the least bit scared of what we're going to do with you?" Grimbowl asked.

"Not really, no," Vincent replied. In truth, he simply hadn't made time to worry about it. Currently, all his brain had space for were the consequences of getting home late.

Although, now that he thought about it, being hung from a branch of a soundproofed tree by fantasy creatures who might decide to kill him wasn't exactly a cakewalk.

"You're even dumber than I thought," Grimbowl said. "Are you sure he's the one you saw, Plimpton?"

"Yes," said a voice from behind Grimbowl. "He's the one from that school science fair."

Vincent's eyes were adjusting to the dark, and he could make out Grimbowl's form standing on a platform built into the tree. The new speaker appeared from the shadows behind Grimbowl, and he moved to stand beside him.

"He looked right at me, saw me," Plimpton went on. "He must be one of the more open-minded humans."

"Then he is perfect," said another voice, and a third elf joined the group.

"Who are you?" Vincent asked. The new elf sounded wise and old, just like the one who'd konked him with the fairy dust.

"I," the wise, old elf said, "am Optar, the tribal advisor to Chief Megon."

"Hooray for you," Vincent said. "Will you let me down now?"

"No," Optar said. "We have need of a human agent, someone to interact with your world in ways that we cannot. You shall be that agent."

"What if I say no?" Vincent said, though he suspected he had very little choice in the matter.

"To ensure your compliance," Optar said, "we shall administer an obyon."

"A what?" Vincent asked. He could see that something sat in the palm of Optar's hand. He couldn't see what it was, but there was definitely something there.

"An obyon," Grimbowl said, "is a magical creature that we put inside your body."

"It monitors your thoughts," Optar said, "and corrects you if you disobey us."

"Corrects me?" Vincent said.

"Remember when I kicked your leg?" Grimbowl said. "This is worse. A lot worse."

"With an obyon in your body, you cannot defy or betray us," Optar said, walking forward and extending the something toward Vincent's face. "Hold still, it won't hurt going in."

"No way!" Vincent said, swinging himself away from the elves. "You're not sticking anything in me."

"It's either this," Grimbowl said, "or we leave you here until you die."

Vincent stopped struggling. This was a bad situation, and it was only going to get worse. However, if he didn't let them do this, he most certainly would not make it home before his family did.

"Okay, get it over with," he said, closing his eyes and waiting.

Vincent felt something attach to his cheek, then crawl over to his nose.

"It's a bug?" he asked as it entered his left nostril.

"A ladybug," Optar said, "treated to our magical specifications. Any insect can be used to create an obyon."

"Except roaches," Grimbowl said. "They lay their eggs up there, and then you get bugs crawling out of your nose all the time."

Vincent thought he was going to be sick. The obyon climbed up his nasal passage, and settled itself far at the back.

"Why don't we test it?" Optar suggested. "Give the lad a taste of what he's in for if he disobeys us."

"That's okay!" Vincent said. "Really."

"No, it's a good idea," Grimbowl said. "Go ahead, Vincent. Do something disobedient."

"This really isn't necessary…"

"Yes it is, Vincent," Grimbowl said. "I order you to disobey me."

"No!" Vincent replied. "I won't…aaagh!"

The pain was like a red-hot poker exploding behind his eyes. Vincent had never in his life felt so much agony, and he had no desire to feel it again. Not that he'd desired it the first time.

"That was a laugh," Grimbowl said.

"No it was not," Vincent replied, redoubling his efforts to break free. "I did my part; I let you stick that thing in me. Now let me go!"

"I order you not to struggle," Optar said, and Vincent stopped instantly.

"Fast learner," Grimbowl said. "Hey kid, I order you to struggle."

"What?" Vincent cried. Then, "Ow!" when he didn't immediately obey. He struggled, hoping the pain would stop, but it did not. The elves had given him conflicting orders; he couldn't possibly comply with them both.

"I order you to stretch your arms out!" Optar said.

"I order you to do jumping jacks!" Grimbowl added.

"I order you to do the waltz! With me!"

Vincent tossed back and forth, screaming himself hoarse, wishing he were dead. The two elves continued to toss conflicting or impossible orders at him, and he thought his head would explode.

"That's enough."

The voice was deep and full of authority. Vincent looked in its direction, and saw an elf on the branch below him.

"Hello, Vincent," the new elf said. "I am Chief Megon. I see that my fellow elves have successfully inserted an obyon into your nasal cavities. Do you understand what we want from you?"

"Yeah," Vincent replied, the pain in his head waning. "You want me to be your slave."

"I would prefer to think of you as an ally," Chief Megon said. "Albeit one who cannot be otherwise."

"So what do you want me to do?" Vincent asked.

"Grimbowl will contact you when we require your services," Megon said. "Optar, release him."

"Yes, chief," Optar said, and he uttered some words that Vincent couldn't understand.

Then, the grass ropes binding Vincent suddenly lost their magic. Devoid of their strength, they could no longer hold Vincent's weight. With several snaps they gave, and Vincent plummeted to the ground below.

"Don't hit the ground!" Grimbowl called after him.

Vincent Drear staggered home as fast as he could. One hand clutched at his head, the other at his sore rump.

Vincent supposed he should have considered himself lucky. He could have easily broken his neck after his head-first fall from the elves' tree. Instead, he'd dropped down into a hedge, then fell from that to a harsh landing on his bum. Then, because he hit the ground against Grimbowl's wishes, the obyon up his nose had launched another massive dose of pain.

When he'd been able, Vincent had picked himself up and hobbled in the direction of home. The elves' laughter followed him, and Vincent resisted the urge to throw a rock at their tree. Who knew how much pain he'd have to endure if he did that.

His number-one priority was to get home before his family, if that was still possible. Vincent walked as fast as he could, unable to run because of his sore bum.

While he walked, Vincent had time to consider the implications of what had been done to him. He had a magical bug living inside his nose, put there by a race Chanteuse had described as mischievous. As long as that bug was up there, the elves could make him do whatever they wanted.

What if they asked him to gnaw off his arms? Or told him to kill someone? He was totally under their control for as long as the obyon lived.

How long did obyons live? And what (gulp) did they eat?

"Steady on, Vincent," he told himself as he hobbled. "There has to be a way out of this. Think!"

He thought. And while he did so, he followed the bike path out of the park and turned left. Now he only had a few blocks to go before he was safe and sound.

"I could blow it out!" Vincent thought, and he dug around in his pocket for a tissue. He had none, so he pulled up his shirt bottom and tried that.

Several blows later, he realized it was hopeless. The obyon was anchored too tightly to simply be blown out.

"Wait a minute," Vincent snapped his fingers. "It's an insect, right? I could squirt some bug spray up my nose!"

He walked a few more meters feeling very happy before he remembered that bug spray was poisonous.

"Darn!" he said, his spirits dropping again. It was a moot point, anyway; his parents believed in the sanctity of all life, and so there wasn't any bug spray in the house.

"If I just took a small dose," he wondered aloud. "I could go over to Big Tom's place and use some there. I know they have some…"

Big Tom's home was practically an insect hive. Every time Vincent went over, he spent a good deal of his time helping the family spray roaches. They had boxes of big, black cans in their basement, each with large and foreboding symbols on the front. Breathing the stuff in was not recommended.

"Too big a risk," he said as he turned the corner onto his street. "There must be something else I can do. Maybe if I stuck something up my nose…"

"Who's he talking to?"

"Himself, I think."

Vincent couldn't say for sure if he'd really heard the voices or not. They'd been so faint, just on the edge of his hearing. He looked up and saw the sign for his street above him, with two tiny people sitting upon it.

"What gives?" he said. "All of a sudden, there are weird critters everywhere!"

The two tiny people stood up, and golden wings unfolded behind their backs.

"He sees us!" one of them said.

"No, I didn't!" Vincent said hastily, backing away quickly. "No need to stick a bug up my nose. I'm leaving!"

With that, he turned and ran. Fast.

• • •

Vincent had already slammed the front door behind him when he remembered he was supposed to be quiet. It had been his intention to sneak back into the house and re-seal himself in the chapel, just on the off chance his parents hadn't checked up on him when they'd arrived home.

And they were home. In his flight from the tiny winged people, Vincent had nevertheless noticed the car was back in the driveway. If he was lucky, they might have gone straight to bed. If he was unlucky…

Vincent heard a commotion upstairs in his parents' bedroom. They were coming to investigate! Vincent moved quickly, ignoring his pained bottom as he hurried to the basement. They were in their room, so they probably didn't know he'd been out. If they did know, he reasoned, they would have stayed up and waited for him to come home. If he could get to the chapel before he was seen, he might just get away with it yet.

Vincent hopped off the last stair and made for the still-ajar chapel doors. Upstairs, he could hear his father's footsteps coming down the stairs to the front door. Would he check the basement? Let's not wait around to find out, Vincent told himself as he carefully opened the chapel door and slipped inside. Using extra care, Vincent set the door back on its hinge and backed away.

"Whew," he whispered, sitting back down on the cold concrete floor.

He'd made it. Through pure good fortune, and perhaps a bit of divine help, Vincent had managed to escape his parents' wrath. They hadn't checked the basement when they'd gotten home, and if they did now they would find nothing out of the ordinary.

He was home free.

Suddenly, a bright light blazed into his eyes. Blinded, Vincent held a hand in front of his face. Through his fingers, he could just make out the form of his brother Max sitting before him, holding a flashlight. Max's face was cold and hard, and full of Righteousness.

"You are in very big trouble," Max said.

"Oh, no," Vincent said, although "oh no" didn't really cover it. All his brother had to do was yell, and their father would hear and come to investigate.

"You were told to remain here until morning," Max said, "as Penance for your lack of Faith today. Instead you escaped, and were up to Triumvirate knows what!"

"Shh!" Vincent hissed, his mind racing. What could he possibly say to keep his brother quiet?

"Honor thy father and mother!" Max raged at him.

"Shh!" Vincent repeated. "What are you doing here?"

"I was waiting for you to return," Max said, "so I could catch you, and see how you'd escaped. Now I know, I'll make sure Mother and Father never let it happen again."

"What if I told you," Vincent said, thinking fast, "that I was on a mission for the Triumvirate?"

"I don't believe you," Max said. "You're trying to save yourself from the consequences of your sin."

"I am not!" Vincent lied, knowing full well that he was. "How do you think I got out of here?" He calmed himself, desperate to keep his voice down. "The Triumvirate told me the door was unhinged. I swear on my life!"

"Go on," Max said, his face a fraction less severe.

He's buying it, Vincent thought, and he went on.

"They told me to spend my penance time in Their service to make up for today," he said, making sure to pronounce the capital "T" on "Their." "They wanted me to go to the park and look for devil creatures."

At that, Vincent felt a tiny pang of pain from the obyon. It was a warning; he'd been ordered not to talk about the elves.

However, nobody had said anything about those tiny winged guys. They were fair game, and were about to get him out of trouble.

"I went to the park to investigate," Vincent went on, "and I saw a bunch of little people," his headache increased, "with tiny wings on their backs." The headache subsided. "When they saw me, they attacked and held me prisoner in the trees."

"No we didn't!"

Vincent jumped, then spun around. Hovering in the air behind him were the two little people he'd seen on the street sign. Their wings buzzed like dragonflies and glowed like lightning bugs.

"He's telling lies about us, Clara," the male one said to the female. "Talking about us as if we were elves!"

"How did you get in here?" Vincent asked them.

"We followed you," Clara said.

"You nearly squashed us when you slammed that door," the male said. "And now you're telling lies! I ought to rip your head off right now."

"Calm down, Nod," Clara said. "He probably doesn't know what we are." She looked up at Vincent. "You haven't seen post-Epoch beings before, have you?"

"Post what?" Vincent asked.

"Who," Max asked, "are you talking to?"

"These guys," Vincent said, moving out of the way so that Clara and Nod would be in full view.

"What guys?" Max said.

"Come on, they're glowing!" Vincent said, waving a hand at the tiny creatures. "You must see something."

"I don't see…anything," Max said, but his eyes told a different story. He saw something, all right. He just didn't know what to make of it. Vincent knew that Max, like his parents, believed in supernatural creatures. For a Triumvirite, it was something of a prerequisite. There were angels above and demons below; what would his mind end up deciding?

"All I see is your sin," Max said, blinking and shaking his head. Clearly, he'd chosen to see nothing.

"Max..." Vincent began, while Nod and Clara sighed.

"You are making up stories about demonic creatures," Max went on, "and daring to suggest that the Triumvirate sent you on a quest. You really think I'd believe you?"

"It was a long shot," Vincent said.

"We don't have time for this guy," Nod said, and he flew at Max at high speed.

"Stop!" Vincent cried, lunging after him. His brother wasn't his favorite person, but he didn't want Max hurt.

"Hey!" said Nod as Vincent grabbed hold of his tiny legs.

"Woah!" said Vincent as the little man dragged him forward.

"What are you doing?" Max asked, his face awash in puzzlement.

"Let go of him!" Clara said. She flew above Vincent, then drove both her feet down into his back.

"Oof!" Vincent said as the wind was clobbered from his lungs.

"Woah!" cried Nod as Vincent's hands suddenly released him, and he sped out of control into Max's chest.

"Yunnng!" cried Max as he and Nod flew backward into the altar behind him, knocking it over with a loud crash.

"Nod!" Clara cried, leaping off of Vincent and flying after her companion.

"Oww…" Vincent moaned, lying in a crumpled heap. He hurt all over, and didn't want to move ever again. He'd been through enough today, and he prayed it wouldn't get any worse.

"What is going on in here?" said Vincent's father, throwing open the chapel door.

"Oh no," Vincent muttered.

Things had just gotten worse.

"What on God's green pastures?" Vincent's father said, staring around the chapel. Light from the basement illuminated the scene of chaos before him, but all his attention was focused on the two tiny winged people.

He sees them, Vincent realized.

"Back, foul beasts of the Devil!" Mr. Drear roared,

grabbing the cross around his neck and thrusting it as far as its chain would allow. "In the name of the Triumvirate, I command you…"

"Shut up," Nod said, and he flew right up to Mr. Drear and biffed him on the chin.

"Stop!" Vincent cried, leaping up and catching his father as he fell. He was out cold; Vincent laid him gently down on the floor of the chapel, then rounded on the flying figure.

"Stop hitting my family!" he said, poking a finger into Nod's chest.

"Touch me again," Nod said dangerously, "and you'll lose that finger, buddy."

"Oh really?" Vincent said, and he drove his other fist into the tiny man's entire body. Nod flew back and bounced off the wall, then spiraled down to the floor.

"Nod!" Clara cried, then she flew at Vincent. "You'll pay, human!"

Vincent was ready for her. He spun out of Clara's way, and when she stopped to turn back he bopped her hard on her tiny head.

"Ow!" Clara said, then she grabbed Vincent's hand and twisted. Vincent flipped through the air, then landed upside down on his unconscious brother.

"I'll fix you up," Clara said, grabbing Vincent by the leg and lifting him into the air. "I hope you like the wall, because you're going to be a part of it!"

She swung Vincent around in an arc, but when she let go something grabbed him and set him down.

"Nod!" Clara cried. "What are you doing?"

"I kinda like this kid," Nod said, landing in front of Vincent. "He's tough, stands up for himself. Gotta respect that. Plus, he can see us." Nod turned and looked up at Vincent. "People like you are in short supply, kid. Sorry about your family. No hard feelings?"

Vincent had some very hard feelings, but didn't think he should push his luck. It had been stupid to pick a fight with these creatures, and the last thing he needed were more fantastical enemies.

"Sure," he said. "And I can understand you two being upset when I called you devil creatures."

"Yeah, what was that all about?" Clara asked, landing next to Nod.

"I had to tell my brother something," Vincent said. "And I couldn't tell him about the creatures who really did attack me," he tapped his nose, "so I used you guys. How was I to know you would follow me home?"

"He's got an obyon," Clara said to Nod. "That's not good."

"They never are," Nod replied, then turned back to Vincent. "Had a run-in with the elves, did you? Nasty bunch, they are. Not as bad as centaurs, but still bad news. No wonder you ran from us. Things haven't been going your way, have they?"

"No," Vincent agreed. "Look, before we talk further, can you two help me out? I'd really rather my dad and brother didn't wake up in here and freak out all over again. Help me get them upstairs, then we can talk all you want."

The small creatures continued to surprise and amaze Vincent with their strength. Nod carried Mr. Drear back upstairs without any help at all, and Clara was just fine carrying Max. While the tiny ones laid his family back in their beds, Vincent grabbed some snacks from the kitchen and returned to the Chapel.

They talked, and they ate chips and drank caffeine-free diet cola. Vincent learned that Clara and Nod were pixies, who, like the elves, had recently settled in the neighborhood. Vincent also learned that there were many fantasy-type creatures now living within the city's limits.

"It's a regular fantasapalooza out there," Nod said. "And more come in every day."

"How come?" Vincent asked, taking a big gulp from his bottle of cola. His parents insisted he and Max only enjoy soft drinks when entertaining guests. Well, the pixies were guests, weren't they?

"You don't know?" Nod said.

"Of course he doesn't know," Clara said. "He only started seeing our kind today. But I'm sure he knows about the Portal Site."

"The what?" Vincent asked, shoveling chips into his mouth. The chips were also strictly for guests, but Vincent had missed his supper.

"You know, Portal Sites," Clara said.

"No, I don't," Vincent replied.

Clara stared at him in open-mouthed shock for what felt like a full minute. Nod sighed and shook his head.

"You really don't know?" Clara asked.

"No," Vincent replied. "I don't. And you are starting to seriously annoy me. What is a Portal Site?"

The two pixies turned and looked at each other.

"Should we tell him?" Clara asked. "I mean, if he doesn't know…"

"None of them know," Nod said. "It's like I've been telling you, something is messed up this time around. None of the humans know."

"But they must know," Clara said. "It's nearly time, and…"

"Do you see anyone preparing?" Nod said. "Do you see the humans in a mass exodus to the Sites? No, you don't. They don't know. It's like what happened to us, but worse because they don't know."

"Will one of you please tell me what you are talking about!" Vincent said, raising his voice as loud as he dared.

"Vincent," Nod said, "what I'm about to tell you is big. Bigger than anything you've ever heard before."

"I've heard a lot," Vincent said, trying to put on a brave front. Inside, the suspense was eating him alive.

"You haven't heard this," Nod said. "Kid, the world's about to end."

Vincent blinked. His mind absorbed the information, and he was more than a little disappointed.

"That's it?" Vincent asked.

"What do you mean, that's it?" Nod said, kicking a potato chip at him. "The world's going to end. Soon! Doesn't that bother you?"

"I just presented a school project on the end of the

world for our science fair," Vincent told him, "and my parents' church has been telling us we're in the Last Days ever since I was born. I'm sorry, Nod, but the end of the world isn't that big of a shock."

"Wow," Clara said, turning to her companion. "And you say our lives are depressing."

"I do not," Nod said. "Well, sometimes."

"So, how's it going to end?" Vincent asked. "Nuclear war? An asteroid impact? Ice age? Killer bees?"

"Worse," Nod said. "Demons."

"Demons?" Vincent said, the old dread returning. "They actually exist?"

"Not the way you're probably thinking," Nod said. "For one thing, they don't use pitchforks. They don't need them."

"And they're not from Hell," Clara added. "They're part of a natural cleansing process of the Earth."

"Say what?" Vincent said.

"Their purpose," Clara explained, "is to destroy the dominant species whose epoch has passed. It's the only way to prepare the world for the next species."

"You do not want to be stuck behind when the demons come," Nod said. "You see, kid, every few thousand years or so the planet needs to rejuvenate itself.

Have a fresh start. The demons are part of that process. So are the Portal Sites. First you'll get some earthquakes, then some really bad weather, then volcanoes, and then the portals close and the demons come out. It's all about clearing the dominant species off the planet."

"Clearing off…" Vincent said. "You mean a bunch of demons are gonna come to wipe out all humanity?"

"That's about the size of it, yep," Nod replied.

The fact that Vincent did not sleep had nothing to do with the cold concrete floor. His mind reeled with the information he'd been given, alternating between terror and fascination.

The pixies had stayed an extra hour, during which

they'd filled in a few gaps. Specifically, they'd told Vincent about the Portal Sites.

The near future wasn't all bleak. Portal Sites, the pixies explained, were humanity's ticket off the doomed planet.

"When each epoch comes to an end," Nod said, "portals appear at certain sites all over the planet. The creatures who make up that epoch's dominant species are called psychically to those sites, where they can walk through the portals and leave this world behind."

"Where do they go?" Vincent asked.

"Don't know," Clara replied. "We missed our chance to find out. Which is not something I would recommend."

"The portals only stay open for a short time," Nod told him. "Anyone left on the planet after they close is demon food."

"Right now, all of humanity should be stampeding toward the nearest gate," Clara told him. "The fact that you aren't means there's something seriously wrong."

"How come you two didn't get to a portal?" Vincent asked.

"Well, there's a fun story," Nod said. "Basically, it was all because of the centaurs."

"You mentioned centaurs before," Vincent said. "Who are they?"

"Pains in the rear," Nod said. "Thought they were better than any other species."

"They, like us, come from the last epoch," Clara said. "When our time ended six thousand years ago, the centaurs refused to go."

"They thought the planet belonged to them," Nod added, "and figured they were powerful enough to fight the demons off. Boy, were they wrong."

"Just a second," Vincent said. "Are you telling me you are six thousand years old?"

"Nine thousand, actually," Nod said. "And Clara here is eight thousand, though she doesn't look a day over a millennium."

"Thank you, Nod," Clara said. "We have longer lifespans, Vincent. All creatures from our epoch do."

"Wow," Vincent said. "So you were there, fighting the demons with the centaurs?"

"Hell, no!" Nod said. "We wanted off-planet, same as every other species. Problem was, the centaurs wouldn't let us."

"They blocked all the portals," Clara said, "and fought with anyone who tried to get through. A few made it past them, but not many. Centaurs are very powerful magic users, Vincent. When Nod and I tried to get past them, they knocked us back easily."

"Why didn't they want you going through?" Vincent asked.

"Because they're jerks," Nod said.

"Because of balance," Clara clarified. "Each species has its role to play in the natural order of things. The centaurs wanted the world to stay just the way it was."

"But it didn't, right?" Vincent said.

"Nope," Nod replied. "The demons hunted down and killed every last one of them, and most of every other race as well."

"And that's what will happen to you," Clara added, "if you don't find the portals soon."

"Sorry to dump all this on you, kid," Nod added. "We'll tell you if we find the Portal Site, but if we can't...well, good luck to all of us."

After the pixies departed, Vincent sorted through the information they'd given him. A hundred new questions burned in his mind, and all of it came down to one thing; the world was going to end, and soon.

As he lay on the floor of the chapel, mulling it all

over in his mind, he realized he had to do something about it. But what?

"I must talk with Chanteuse again," he said. "She'll know what to do."

• • •

When the Chapel doors finally opened (the proper way), Vincent braced himself for what was to come. His father and brother might have woken up believing that the previous night's excitement had been a dream, but Vincent couldn't count on that.

Before they'd left, the pixies had helped him restore the Chapel to its former pristine state. The altar stood once more, the pop bottles were gone and even the smallest of chip crumbs had been picked off the floor. There was no sign that anyone other than Vincent had been in the Chapel all night, and certainly no evidence that he'd enjoyed himself.

No evidence except my brother and father's memories, Vincent thought as he turned around to face the music.

Instead of his father or Max, however, Vincent saw his mother. He blinked in surprise even as he shielded his eyes from the bright basement light.

"I trust you've learned your lesson?" his mother said.

"Indeed I have," Vincent said, expecting some kind of lecture.

"Good," his mother said. "Come along and have breakfast. I made pancakes."

Vincent blinked with surprise once more. What was all this about?

"What is all this about?" Vincent asked as he followed his mother back upstairs.

"I thought you deserved a treat after spending all night in the Chapel," she replied.

"You did?" Vincent said, his surprise growing as he sat down at the kitchen table. His mother had already made the pancakes, and had even got out the 100% pure maple syrup. They only ever used that on Christmas morning, yet there it was.

"Yes, I did," his mother said, sitting down across from him. "Can a mother not spoil her child every now and then?"

"I thought the Triumvirate didn't allow that sort of thing," Vincent said, eyeing her suspiciously. That had certainly been his parents' policy up until now.

"I thought so, too," his mother replied, serving up the pancakes, "but an angel told me differently last night."

Vincent, who'd been reaching for the syrup, stopped.

"Angel?" he asked.

"Yes, I awoke last night to see an angel putting your father back to bed," his mother said. "He said the Triumvirate were angry with the way we'd been treating you."

"Did he?" Vincent said, smiling inwardly. That cheeky little pixie!

"He said I should spoil you," his mother said, "so that's what I am doing."

Vincent thought this was jolly good fun, but then he saw the look in his mother's eyes. She looked scared, very much so. Vincent guessed she was feeling the same fear he'd felt when he'd seen his first elf. Of course, his mother believed in angels and demons. But it was quite another thing to actually see one.

"Um, thanks," Vincent said, pouring the syrup. "This is great, mom."

"Is there anything else I can do for you?" his mother asked, her voice just a tiny bit frantic. "A glass of milk? Or would you like to try coffee?"

"No thanks, I'm good," Vincent said, tucking into his pancakes. They were a little tough and lumpy; his mother never did learn the art of pancake cooking.

"How are they, dear?" she asked, her voice cracking with tension.

"Fine, just great," Vincent said quickly, taking another mouthful and giving her the thumbs up.

Man, he thought, *this is starting to freak me out. What did Nod say to her?*

"What did the angel say to you, Mom?" Vincent asked. "You seem a little wigged."

"You would be too if you'd seen an angel," his mother replied. "Although I did expect him to be a bit bigger…well." She got up suddenly. "I'd better see if your father and brother are up yet."

Uh oh, thought Vincent, who'd almost forgotten the trouble he might face if his father and Max had any recollection of the previous night. Maybe Nod had said something to them as well? No, Max hadn't been able to see the pixies, not really. And his dad had thought they were demons. Curious, Vincent thought, that his mother saw them as angels. Perhaps people saw them the way they wanted to.

His mother left the kitchen and hurried upstairs. If he didn't know better, Vincent might have thought she was now afraid of him. Vincent wasn't sure he knew better. He wolfed down his remaining pancakes, then walked quickly to the front door and put on his shoes. He would have loved to change his clothes, as his previous day's clothes were feeling a bit sticky, but Vincent wanted to avoid his family if he could possibly help it.

It was a school day, but with the world ending Vincent thought he might take a day off. If he hurried, he might be able to intercept Chanteuse before she left for her own school. He would tell her everything that had happened to him in the last twelve hours, and fill her in on Portal Sites and ending epochs and so on.

Vincent put his jacket on, and was turning the door handle when he heard someone coming down the stairs. A moment later Max appeared, still dressed in his clothes from yesterday. He looked wiped out, as if he'd slept too much, but when he saw Vincent he straightened immediately.

"Vincent!" he said. "Where do you think you're going?"

"School," Vincent replied, opening the door. "Gotta go. Bye."

Vincent slammed the door in his brother's face, then ran off down the street.

Chanteuse was meditating on her front lawn as Vincent approached. Great, he thought. I haven't missed her.

"Hold it right there, kid."

Vincent spun around and looked down. Grimbowl stood on the sidewalk behind him, wearing his usual cheeky smile.

"You wouldn't be thinking of telling our mutual friend about last night's goings-on," Grimbowl asked, "would you?"

"That is exactly what I plan to do," Vincent said, and he resumed his walk to Chanteuse's house.

"Stop," Grimbowl said.

Pain erupted in Vincent's head, so he stopped.

"You will not," Grimbowl said, "tell Chanteuse anything about our little talk. Do you get me?"

Vincent stared daggers at the elf, who smiled back in a smug way.

"I get you," Vincent said. "I was going to talk to her about something else."

"Forget it. It's time for you to go to work," Grimbowl said. "Come with me."

Vincent was torn. He wanted very badly to talk to Chanteuse, but he knew the price of disobedience only too well. He took one last look at his meditating friend, then hurried off after the elf.

• • •

It was only a few minutes before Vincent realized the elf was leading him to school. That irritated him to no end, since he'd all but decided to skip today's classes. A good education was important, or so he'd been told many times over by his parents, his teachers, and his brother. Right now, though, doing something about the end of the world seemed just a tad more urgent than math and geography.

They reached the edge of the school's football field and headed for the parking lot. Grimbowl pointed as a limo pulled into the lot, and Vincent watched as the school's richest kid got out.

"Barnaby Wilkins," he said with a full dose of contempt.

"You know him?" Grimbowl said. "Good. That'll make things easier."

"You want me to beat him up?" Vincent asked hopefully, the memory of Big Tom's bruises still fresh in his mind.

"Nope," Grimbowl said. "We want you to make friends with him."

"Oh come on!" Vincent said. "You want me to hang out with that jerk?"

"Yes," Grimbowl replied.

"I won't do it."

"Oh yes you will," Grimbowl replied. "If you don't want your head to explode, you'll do exactly what I say."

Vincent grunted but made no further comment. The elf was right and he knew it.

"I'm right," Grimbowl said. "And you know it."

"Okay, fine, I'll make friends with Barnaby," Vincent said. "But why? What do you care about some rich kid?"

"You remember my buddy Plimpton?" Grimbowl said. "He got a look at the science fair project Barnaby did, the one on government conspiracies. We think he might be on to something. You ever hear of the Portal Sites?"

"Portal Sites?" Vincent said. "What are those?" If he admitted he knew about Portal Sites, Grimbowl would have wanted to know how, and Vincent didn't want the elves knowing about his meeting with the pixies if he could help it. He had the feeling the two groups didn't exactly get along.

"So you think the government is hiding these Portal Sites?" Vincent said when Grimbowl had finished explaining.

"That's what you're going to find out," Grimbowl said. "Go make friends with him, find out where he got the idea for his project, then tell me what he knows. Got it?"

"Sure, whatever," Vincent said. "Why didn't you stick a bug up his nose?"

"Because…because we got you first," the elf said. "Boy, you ask a lot of questions. You know what? No more questions, kid."

"But what…aarg!"

"That's right," Grimbowl said. "That's what you get. Now stop rolling around on the ground clutching your head and go make friends with Barnaby."

When he was able, Vincent got back up and headed for the school parking lot. Barnaby was still there, chatting away with his two bodyguards, Bruno and Boots.

"I can't believe I'm doing this," Vincent muttered as he approached his enemy. "Somehow, I've got to get that bug out of my nose."

Barnaby saw him coming, and immediately alerted his bodyguards to Vincent's presence. Vincent thought hard, trying to think what to say. How, exactly, do you make friends with someone you hate? What would they possibly have to talk about?

"Hey, Barnaby," Vincent said, stopping two meters short of him. "What's new?"

Barnaby stared at him in momentary bewilderment. Vincent took that as a good sign and kept going.

"Nice day, huh?" he said, trying to effect a genuine smile.

"What," Barnaby said, "do you want?"

"Nothing," Vincent said, eyeing the bodyguards. Their expressions were unreadable under their shades, but Vincent had the distinct impression they wanted to do him harm. All it would take was one word from Barnaby, and they'd be on him.

"Get him," Barnaby said.

Okay, maybe two words.

"Wait!" Vincent cried as Bruno grabbed him by his shirt and hefted him into the air. "I wanted to talk about your science fair project."

"What about it?" Barnaby asked, watching with amusement as his minder turned Vincent upside down and held him by his foot.

"It was really good," Vincent said as he swung from Bruno's hand. That's twice now I've been up-ended because of the elves, he thought. I don't like it, not at all.

"Of course it was good!" Barnaby said. "I had the best display, the latest cutting-edge technology, the most plausible end-of-the-world scenario."

"I know," said Vincent. "But I didn't get a chance to really look at it, because I was stuck at my own table.

I just wanted to know if I could have a look at your project."

Barnaby appeared to be considering Vincent's plea. He's buying it, Vincent thought. Now's the time to move in for the kill.

"I know we haven't always seen eye-to-eye," Vincent said, "but I want to change all that. I think we could be friends."

"Friends?" Barnaby said with a laugh. "Me, friends with a loser like you?"

"Hey, I didn't think much of you, either," Vincent said, "until I saw that project of yours," he added hastily as Bruno gave his ankle a sharp squeeze. "I realized there's more to you than meets the eye. Give me a chance, you'll see there's more to me, too."

Barnaby thought about it. Vincent hung patiently, his fingers crossed for luck.

"No," Barnaby said. "Get lost, loser."

"Just a moment, Barnaby."

Vincent, Barnaby, and the two bodyguards turned to the limo. A middle-aged man with slicked-back gray hair and a business suit had just rolled down the car's back window.

"You can't fault the boy for having taste in friends," the man said, "though he clearly has none in clothing."

Barnaby laughed at that. So did Bruno and Boots. Vincent faked a smile, but laughter was just a tiny bit beyond him.

"That's my dad," Barnaby said. "He's one of the top executives at Alphega Corp."

"Francis Wilkins," said Barnaby's dad. "I'd shake your hand, but…"

"…I'm a little hung up right now?" Vincent finished for him.

"Why don't you give this boy a chance?" Mr. Wilkins said, winking at his son. Barnaby smiled and nodded back.

Uh oh, Vincent thought.

Mr. Wilkins rolled up his window, and the limo pulled out of the school parking lot. Barnaby made a hand gesture, and Bruno dropped Vincent to the pavement.

"Okay, you'll get a chance," Barnaby said. "But first I've got a job for you, to prove you really are a guy I can be seen with."

"Yeah?" Vincent said, getting back up and rubbing his head. "What would that be?"

"Beat up on someone for me."

"Beat someone up?" Vincent said.

"You scared to pick a fight?" Barnaby asked, and his bodyguards snickered.

"No, I am not," Vincent replied.

"Good," said Barnaby. "Then beat up on your friend Big Tom."

Lunch hour. High noon, as it were. Vincent walked slowly around the side of the school, with Big Tom following closely behind.

"So what's this thing you want to show me?" his best friend asked.

"It's just around here," Vincent replied, staring straight ahead.

He couldn't believe he was doing this. All through morning classes he'd dreaded this moment, and now that it was here he wanted to throw up.

He was really going to do it. He was going to beat up his best friend.

"Is it really special?" Big Tom asked.

"Sort of," Vincent replied.

"Will it knock my socks off?" Big Tom asked.

Vincent groaned.

"We'd better be careful," Big Tom said. "This is where that jerk Barnaby takes kids he wants to beat up."

"You don't say."

"It's 'cause the teachers don't patrol around here," Big Tom went on. "Nobody'd see you if you got beat up."

"Uh huh," Vincent said, turning around. They were far enough away now. Big Tom was right; no one would see.

Almost no one. From around the side of the school Vincent could see Barnaby and his two bodyguards. Vincent had told Barnaby he would beat up Big Tom at lunch hour, and there Barnaby was to make sure he did it.

"So where's the thing?" Big Tom asked, looking up at his best friend with his big and soppy puppy-dog eyes.

Vincent looked back down at his friend. Could he really go through with this? Did he actually have to? Vincent had tried to work out another option all morning, but had come up blank. The order Grimbowl had given him was to make friends with Barnaby. Barnaby's condition was that he had to beat up Big Tom. Vincent knew that if he didn't do it, didn't gain Barnaby's friendship, his head would explode with pain.

There was no way out. He had to do it.

"You have to do it, kid."

Vincent's head snapped around and down. Grimbowl stood two meters behind him, watching.

"What is it?" Big Tom asked. "Is it the thing?"

"It is the thing," Vincent said, having a sudden brainstorm. In one swift motion he grabbed Big Tom in a headlock and clamped a hand over his eyes.

"Hey!" Big Tom said. "What're you…"

"Shh," Vincent said. "You'll scare him."

"Him?"

"A magical creature," Vincent said. "Like something out of a fantasy movie. And it's standing right in front of you."

"Kid?" Grimbowl said. "What are you doing?"

"He'll talk to you, if you listen just right," Vincent said.

"Really?" said Big Tom.

"Vincent…" Grimbowl said.

"What was that?" Big Tom asked.

Perfect, Vincent thought. He believes he's going to see something. He can even hear Grimbowl now.

"Take a look," Vincent said, and he removed his hand from Big Tom's eyes.

Big Tom stared. Then he stared some more. Grimbowl glared up at Vincent, not pleased at all.

"Is that thing…real?" Big Tom asked.

"That thing," the elf said, "is Grimbowl."

Big Tom was so surprised he would have taken a step back, were he not still in Vincent's headlock.

"This doesn't change anything," Grimbowl said. "You still have to beat him up, Vincent."

"What?" Big Tom asked, craning his head around to look at his friend.

"I have to," Vincent replied. "It's…a long story."

"No it isn't," Grimbowl said. "Kid, Vincent has to beat you up so that Barnaby will be friends with him."

"Huh?" said Big Tom. "You wanna be friends with that jerk?"

"It's not like that," Vincent said, looking over his shoulder at the jerk in question. Barnaby looked impatient, and so did Bruno and Boots.

"Let me go!" Big Tom shouted, and he began struggling like anything. Big Tom, apart from being very fast, was also an expert struggler. He'd gotten so good at it that only the two of Barnaby's bodyguards could successfully hold him.

"Quit it," Vincent said, clutching tighter. He knew it was hopeless; in seconds Big Tom would break free and run away, and Vincent wouldn't have a prayer of catching him.

"Vincent," Grimbowl said, "I order you to beat up your friend."

Oh no, Vincent thought. I'm out of options.

Vincent grabbed Big Tom's shirt front with his free hand, pulled him up and around, then drove his knee into his friend's stomach. Big Tom doubled up, and Vincent swung both fists down hard onto the back of his head.

Big Tom collapsed to the ground. Vincent turned

him over, squatted on his chest, and pinned his arms with his knees.

"Vincent, stop," Big Tom moaned.

"I'm sorry," Vincent said, and he swung again.

Vincent had read once that when mass murderers were killing, their minds went off to another place and left their bodies to do the work. He wished that would happen to him. What he was doing made him feel sick to his stomach.

Confident that Big Tom had had enough, Vincent stood back up. Big Tom lay on the ground, crying. His nose was bloody and his left eye was black, not the worst beating he'd ever had. It could have been much worse.

At least, that's what Vincent told himself.

"Bravo!" cried Barnaby, clapping his hands as he and Boots walked toward the scene of the fight. "You sure showed that little loser."

"Will you show me your science fair project now?" Vincent said.

"Hell, no!" Barnaby said. "I just wanted to see if you'd actually do it."

The shock on Vincent's face was so delightful to Barnaby that he burst out laughing. Vincent swung a fist at the bully, but Boots grabbed his arm and twisted it behind his back.

"I've got him," the bodyguard said, and Vincent looked up to see Bruno approaching with a teacher. "This is the guy who beat up Thomas."

"Looks like somebody's in trouble," Barnaby said, and he laughed again.

• • •

Vincent sat on the bench outside the office, waiting for judgment. He might get a week's detention, if he was lucky. If he was unlucky, the principal would make an example of him and have him suspended.

But that wouldn't be the worst of it. His parents would be called, and he'd probably spend the rest of his natural life in the Chapel. Which, if what the pixies had said was true, wouldn't be that much longer.

"Boy, am I going to get it," Vincent said.

"You're not wrong there," a familiar voice replied.

Vincent was getting used to voices from behind catching him off guard. He looked up, and saw the pixie Nod hovering above him.

Now what? he thought.

"That couldn't have been pleasant, being ordered

to hurt your friend," Nod said, landing on the bench beside him.

"How do you know about that?" Vincent asked.

"I've been following you," Nod said. "We always follow people who have an obyon in them, in case they're ordered to fight us. You didn't tell the elf about our meeting, did you?"

"Nope," Vincent said. "What he doesn't know won't hurt me."

"Or us," said Nod. "So why did he order you to attack that boy?"

Vincent quickly told the pixie about Barnaby and his project, and his failed attempt to win his trust.

"I don't think it's your government," Nod said when Vincent had finished. "Even if they knew about the Portals, and wanted to hide them, they'd only be able to hide the Portals in this country. But a large corporation, one with offices worldwide, they might have the resources to cover all the Portal Sites up."

"A big company…" Vincent said. "You know, Barnaby's dad works for a really big company called Alphega Corp. Their corporate headquarters are out in Brampton. Could they be hiding the Portal Site?"

"That depends," Nod said. "How big is their head-quarters?"

"Big," Vincent said. "Really big." He remembered the two times his family had driven past the towering structure on their way to the *Titanic* movie theater. They did a lot of protests at the *Titanic*.

"Then we should check it out," Nod said, taking to the air. "Let's go."

Nod flew off toward the nearest exit. Vincent stood up to follow, then hesitated. He was in enough trouble as it was. If he left the school now...

"Priorities," Vincent told himself. "The world is ending, after all."

Satisfied, he hurried after Nod.

The Alphega Corporate Headquarters was a large, impos-
ing building, located in the Toronto suburb of Brampton.
It towered over the surrounding industrial buildings, and
was three times as wide as the nearest warehouse.

"It's a good bet," Nod said, "the portal's in there.
They probably built this building around it."

Vincent nodded but said nothing. His attention was on the main entrance, where two armed guards paced back and forth. Vincent crouched beside a car in the parking lot, which covered even more space than the building itself. It had taken them two hours on several buses to get to the lot's perimeter, and another half an hour to cross it on foot. And it was only when they arrived that they saw a bus dropping people off at the main entrance.

"How was I to know?" Nod had said when confronted with Vincent's foul temper. "I never take the bus."

"We have to find another way in," Vincent said, watching as an employee entered through the main doors. "Look, he had to show those guards a pass, then he had to use another pass to get in the doors."

"Wasn't that the same pass?" Nod asked.

"No," said Vincent. "Definitely a second pass."

"No problem," Nod said. "We'll wait until someone comes out, then beat them up and take their passes."

"I don't think that will work," Vincent said. "Those passes probably have photos on them. Besides, you're a pixie and I'm fourteen. We'll look a bit suspicious."

"Okay, so we beat up the security guards," Nod said.

"That might work," Vincent said, "but look at those security cameras. We wouldn't get very far, even if we did make it inside."

"Well, what do you suggest?" Nod asked. "The ventilation system?"

"That only works in movies," Vincent said. "We need something subtle, something unexpected, something...clever."

"But I like beating people up," Nod said.

"I'm sure you'll get the chance soon," Vincent said. "Listen up. Here's my plan."

• • •

Vincent waited outside in the parking lot while Nod did his stuff. They'd had to wait almost an hour for someone to come, but when a woman approached the two security guards Nod had swung into action. He'd flown along behind her, invisible to the guards, and followed the woman inside.

Perfect, Vincent thought, and he moved into position. Any second now the fire alarms would go off and all the employees would evacuate. When that happened, Vincent would make his way to the side of the building. Nod would smash out a window a few floors up, fly out and disable the nearest cameras, then drop down and pick up Vincent. While all the building's employees were milling about outside, Nod would carry Vincent up to the broken window and they would sneak inside.

And when all the employees returned to the building, well…Vincent hoped he and Nod would be done by then.

So, he waited for the sound of the alarm. He stayed low beside a minivan, watching the front entrance with such intensity that he didn't notice the creature sneaking up behind until it licked him.

"Hey!" Vincent cried, spinning around and kicking the licker.

"Yow!" cried the creature, reeling back and clutching its head. It was an elf-sized creature, round of body with a huge mouth. In fact, most of its body was mouth. It was a red-skinned basketball of a thing with arms, legs, and a tail sprouting out from its sides and back. It would have been funny looking if it weren't for the three rows of jagged teeth.

"What did you do that for?" Vincent said, wiping his leg.

"Oww," the creature said, shaking its head. Which basically meant it shook its entire body. "That really…you can see me!"

"Yeah, and I can kick you," Vincent said, and he did. The creature bounced away, then rolled under a car.

"Good riddance," said Vincent, who was starting to think that fantasy creatures were nothing but trouble. He checked his leg to make sure he wasn't getting a rash, then he turned to see if the guards had heard anything. To his relief, they remained at their posts, oblivious.

"Hey! You!" the creature said, crawling out from under the car. "You'll pay for that, you will. Just because I can't bite you now doesn't mean I can't munch you later."

"What," Vincent asked, "are you talking about?"

"It means I'll remember you, boy," the creature said. "And I will, never fear. We demons have very long memories."

"Well, remember this," Vincent said, raising his boot to kick him again. Then the creature's words got through to him, and he stopped. "You're a demon?"

"Darn tootin'," the demon said. "My name's Rennik. Remember it. I like my prey to know who's eating them."

Vincent remembered all the pixies had told him about demons. They would destroy the world at the end of each epoch to make way for the next species. Vincent put his foot down and backed away. He was so scared he almost didn't hear the faint buzz of the fire alarm, or the sound of hundreds of feet.

"Wha…?" he said. He glanced quickly around the van and saw the Alphega employees evacuating the building. It was time, and he had to move. He looked back at Rennik, but the demon was gone.

"Weird," Vincent said, and he hurried off to meet Nod.

When he got to the side of the building, he found that Nod had not broken a window yet. He also noticed the pixie hadn't deactivated a single camera. Vincent hid behind another car, hoping he hadn't already been seen.

What's keeping him? Vincent wondered as he hid. The plan was so simple, he couldn't have messed it up. Vincent looked back at the entrance, where employees were still filing out. If Nod didn't hurry, they would start to go back in and their opportunity would be lost.

A loud smash made him look up. Nod sped by overhead, moving faster than Vincent had ever seen him go. Vincent wondered for half a moment what the pixie was up to, and then he saw the demon. It flew after Nod on dragonlike wings, and it was gaining.

Vincent got up and ran, not caring if the cameras saw

him as he chased the flying creatures. He kept his eyes focused on the two fliers, desperate not to lose them.

Up above, the demon had almost caught up with Nod. A second before its teeth could clamp down on his legs, Nod turned himself ninety degrees and went straight down. The demon hovered a moment, as if trying to figure out what had happened. Then it looked down, saw the fleeing pixie, and sped after him.

Nod made another last-second ninety-degree turn and flew along the ground under the parked cars. The demon flew above the cars, keeping time with the pixie. Nod made a hard right while under a pickup truck, losing the demon for another second before it picked up the trail again.

"I can taste you now," the demon said, waggling its tongue in the air. "You can't hide from me."

Nod made another turn and sped right between Vincent's feet. Vincent looked up and saw the demon cannonballing toward him. Without thinking he leapt into the air, directly into the demon's path.

The demon slammed into Vincent's chest, and that was the last thing he remembered for a while.

Vincent awoke in a haze of pain. His chest hurt mightily, and his whole body felt weird. He felt light, almost as if he were flying. He opened his eyes to see if he was.

He was.

"Aagh!" he said, staring down at the highway below

him. He was at least a hundred meters up, and traveling at a fair lick of speed.

"Quit your whining," Nod said from behind him. "I won't let you go."

"You're carrying me?" Vincent said. He looked behind and could just see the pixie holding him up by his pants. "I forgot how strong you guys are."

"Yeah, we're pretty tough," Nod said.

"You'd better put me down before someone sees us," Vincent said. "We're over Highway 400. There could be accidents."

"Nobody'll see us," Nod said. "People see what they want to see, and they don't want to see a kid flying above them."

"Oh," Vincent said. It seemed to make sense, even though it didn't really. Chanteuse had told him not many people could see fantasy creatures. A kid being carried by a pixie obviously fit into that category.

Vincent rubbed his chest. It hurt a lot, and he couldn't quite remember why.

"What happened to me?" he asked. "I jumped up to stop that demon…"

"And you did," Nod told him. "Thank you, by the way. You saved my life."

"I did?" Vincent said. It hurt to talk, even to breathe, but he couldn't help himself. "I met a demon in the parking lot earlier. He didn't seem that tough."

"That's because it's still your epoch," Nod said. "Demons can't attack you until your portals drop. They get a magical blast of pain if they try. But when your epoch ends, they become your worst nightmare."

"I thought you said they didn't come until the portals close," Vincent said.

"Most come then," Nod explained, "then they go back where they came from. But some choose to stay on Earth to hunt down those who escaped their wrath. We can't fight them, they're too powerful even for us. All we can do is run, and hope they don't get us. Or taste us."

"Taste you?"

"Yeah, taste us," Nod said. "A demon's tongue is a better tracker than a dog's nose. All he's gotta do is taste a spot where you've been and he can track you for miles."

"Is that what happened in the building?"

"Yeah," Nod said. "That place, it's crawling with them. I stayed hidden behind people and under desks until I thought the coast was clear, then I went for the fire alarm."

"And the coast wasn't clear?"

"Almost. I saw the demon just after I pulled the alarm. It had its tongue out, and it sensed something was up. I hid, but then it licked the alarm handle and got my taste. I had no choice but to make a run for it. And when that thing comes to, it'll come for me."

"Oh, no," Vincent said.

"Don't worry, he'll be out for a while," Nod said. "We've got time. I'll take you home, then I'll have to split."

"Can't the other pixies help you?" Vincent asked.

"Not against a demon," Nod replied. "He'd get their taste, then he'd hunt them all down one at a time. Best if I run alone."

"There's got to be someone who can help you," Vincent said, looking down at the world below. They'd reached the intersection of Dufferin and Steeles, and a large superstore.

An Alphega Corp. superstore.

"That's it!" Vincent said. "Take us down, Nod. The one person who can help you is in there."

• • •

The supermarket was one of the largest Vincent had ever seen. Aisles of foodstuffs stretched as far as the eye could see, in both directions, and fronted with a line of cashiers. Hundreds of customers bustled about this way and that with bags, baskets, and carts, and employees in tacky orange uniforms rushed all around them trying to get their jobs done.

"Does 'needle in a haystack' mean anything to you?" Nod asked as he surveyed the store from his vantage point on Vincent's shoulder.

Vincent didn't answer; he just stood there clutching his chest. The pain had hit him a lot harder when they'd landed in the parking lot, and the walk over had been sheer torture. Nod had said it was a good thing—the more pain Vincent was in, the more pain the demon would be in—but Vincent hadn't found that bit of news comforting.

"This way," he croaked, and staggered forward. "We'll ask, see if she's here, then go find her."

They approached the first cashier. He looked about twenty, worn out, and stressed. He scanned items quickly with exhausted arms, all but throwing them into bags for the customer who stood beside his till. Two large monitors stood above his register; one displayed the scanned items and their prices, and the other remained blank.

"Excuse me?" Vincent said. The cashier ignored him and continued his work.

"Sir?" Vincent tried again, tapping the man's shoulder.

"What?" the cashier spun around quickly, his irritation obvious.

"I need to know if Chanteuse Sloam is working today," Vincent said.

"Yeah, I think so," the cashier said, then he quickly returned to his duty.

"Can you tell me where she is?" Vincent asked.

"I don't know," the cashier said, turning back to Vincent. "She works cash. Just walk up and down here, you're bound to…"

Suddenly, the blank monitor sprang to life. A digitized mock-up of Barnaby Wilkins's dad appeared on the screen, wearing a reproachful frown.

"Robert Landers," said the pixilated Mr. Wilkins, "you are neglecting your customer. A one-hour pay cut will be applied to your account."

"Oh, great," the cashier said as the screen went blank. "Thanks a lot, kid."

Vincent hurried on, feeling guilty. That guy got a pay cut just for talking to him? What kind of insane monsters ran this place? Oh yeah, Alphega Corp.

He approached another cashier, determined to be faster.

"Where is Chanteuse's cash?" he asked a teenage girl who worked just as furiously at her till.

"What?" the girl asked, not taking her eyes off the items in front of her.

"Chanteuse Sloam," Vincent said. "Where is she?"

"Over there somewhere, I think," the girl said hurriedly, waving with her left hand.

"Can we get on with this, please?" the customer asked.

"Sorry, sir," the girl said, not fast enough.

"Bridget Auer," said Mr. Wilkins on the second screen, "your customer has expressed displeasure in your service. This is your third violation today. You are hereby docked a full day's pay."

The girl groaned and began bagging her customer's items. Vincent set off again, following her vague directions.

"Um, kid," said Nod, "I don't suppose you could walk faster? That demon has probably recovered by now, and it'll only take it a few seconds to reacquire my taste."

Vincent groaned and clutched at his chest, but did

manage to walk faster. After all, there was far more at stake than just Nod's life. The world was ending, and the pixie was his best chance to find the Portal, and safety.

To take his mind off the approaching apocalypse, Vincent reviewed the events that had happened at Alphega Corp. and came to a conclusion.

He was pretty sure the demon that had licked him, Rennik, wasn't the same one that had chased Nod. That demon had come from inside the building, whereas Rennik had been in the parking lot. Nod had said the building was crawling with demons, which suggested they were there for a reason.

Most likely, they were guards. And why would a company like Alphega have demons as guards? To keep creatures like pixies and elves far, far away.

Before Vincent could voice that thought, he saw Chanteuse at the cash register in front of him. She was ringing in groceries as fast as the other cashiers, and Vincent had to call her name three times before she heard him and looked around.

"Vincent, hello!" she said. "How lovely to see you. And you have a little friend."

"Yeah, this is Nod," Vincent said, pointing to the pixie on his shoulder. "Nod, meet Chanteuse."

"A pleasure," Nod said.

"Chanteuse Sloam," said Mr. Wilkins on her second screen, "you are neglecting your customer. A one-hour pay cut will be applied to your account."

"Sorry," Vincent said.

"Never mind him," Chanteuse said. "I can tell by your aura something is wrong."

"We need your help," Vincent said. "Can you get away? It's really important."

"Let me finish with this customer," Chanteuse said, "then I will take my break."

Chanteuse scanned the rest of the customer's items, then put up her "cash closed" sign. This did not sit at all well with the line of customers waiting at her cash, especially not the plump woman who'd already put out most of her groceries on the conveyor belt.

"I'm very sorry to inconvenience you," Chanteuse said sweetly. "One of our other cashiers will be more than happy to help you."

"Chanteuse Sloam," said Wilkins, "your customer has expressed displeasure in your service. This is your second violation today. A three-hour pay cut will be applied to your account."

"I don't want to get you in trouble," Vincent said.

"If it is so important that you came here to find me," Chanteuse replied, "then I will make the time for you."

Vincent momentarily forgot his chest pains when he heard that. Very few people would afford him that level of respect. Especially if they were as pretty as Chanteuse.

"Chanteuse Sloam," said the digitized Wilkins, "due to your continuing dereliction of your duty, your manager has been notified. You will..."

"Oh, shush," Chanteuse said, and she switched the screen off.

The superstore had its own café, complete with fast food, fountain drinks, and a large sitting and dining area. After buying two root beers for Vincent and Nod ("You bet I like the stuff! Who doesn't?" Nod had said) and an orange juice for herself, Chanteuse led them over to a table at the back.

"It's a long story..." Vincent began.

"And we don't have time to tell it," Nod interrupted. "I have a demon chasing me, and I need help to shake him. Can you do it?"

"A demon?" Chanteuse said. "Don't be silly. Demons are make-believe."

Just then there was a loud crash, and the ceiling over the cereal aisle caved in. Customers screamed in alarm, but they didn't see the three demons that flew in through the hole. Vincent and Nod did, and from the look on her face they could tell that Chanteuse saw them, too.

The lead demon twirled its tongue in the air, then turned in their direction.

"Those aren't make-believe," Vincent said as the demons came toward them.

As the demons drifted slowly toward the supermarket café, tongues waggling before them like an insect's
antennae, Vincent had time enough to be disappointed.
He'd thought Chanteuse knew everything there was to
know about fantasy creatures, but she hadn't known
about demons. It shook up his world, and he wondered

if she really knew anything. After all, she'd thought that elves were friendly folk before they'd stuck a magical bug up his nose.

He was disappointed, all right, but he was smart enough to know that now was not the time to dwell on such things. They had to do something, and fast.

"We've got to do something," Vincent said. "And fast."

"Vincent…" Chanteuse said, and he could see she was very frightened.

"They can't hurt us," he told her. "Not without hurting themselves. But they can hurt Nod. That's why they're here."

The demons drifted closer, their tongues waving over the crowd that had formed beneath them. The people stared at the hole in the ceiling, oblivious of the creatures that slowly moved in Vincent's direction.

What's taking them so long? Vincent wondered. He'd thought the demons would zoom straight in, when instead they were taking their time. It looked almost like they were searching a dark room, not seeing their target but knowing its rough location.

Vincent looked down at the table, and saw Nod cowering in his cup of root beer. He was in up to his eyes in the fizzy liquid, and Vincent's first thought was that his wings would be all sticky. He looked up and saw the demons, who had stopped three tables away, and he realized something.

The root beer was masking the pixie's taste. Not completely—the demons still knew Nod's general location—but they couldn't get a lock on him. Vincent lowered his head to the cup and whispered urgently.

"Don't move," he said. "Stay in there. I'll get you out of here."

Vincent put the lid back on Nod's cup, sealing him inside. Then he stood up, and motioned for Chanteuse to follow him. They slowly made their way toward the exit, keeping an eye on the hovering demons.

"I might be able to do a cloaking spell," Chanteuse said as they walked. "If it works, it would mask your friend's presence."

"Let's just get out of here," Vincent said. The exit was only a few meters away, but what then? The demons could still track Nod, and they were faster than he was. The pixie would have to spend the rest of his life in the cup, and even that wouldn't be enough. Things looked bad for Nod, all right, but if they made it to the exit he might have a chance.

"Hey! Chanteuse! Where d'you think you're going?"

Vincent turned and saw a tall, thin man with a beard and a frown coming toward them. He didn't need to be told this was Chanteuse's manager. Some things you can just tell.

"Mr. Lunts, I..." Chanteuse began.

"First ya blow off a customer to go talk to your buddy," Mr. Lunts said, "then yer not around to help us keep order during a crisis. Didn't ya see that?" He pointed at the caved-in ceiling without taking his eyes—or his frown—off her.

"I did see..." Chanteuse began.

"Ya saw that, but ya didn't come over to help customers," Mr. Lunts said. "Just too busy talkin' on an unscheduled break with your buddy. Gonna cost ya, little girl."

Vincent looked past Mr. Lunts and saw the demons. They had turned in his direction, and were slowly moving forward.

"We don't have time for this," Vincent said. "Sir, we have..."

"Shut up, kid," Mr. Lunts said. "Chanteuse, what've you got to..."

"Mr. Lunts," Chanteuse said with an intensity that

surprised her manager and Vincent, "there is no call to be rude."

"Don't you interrupt me," Mr. Lunts said, poking a finger at her. "You're in enough trouble."

You don't know the half of it, Vincent thought as he watched the demons approach.

"We have to go," he said, taking Chanteuse's hand.

"You can go, I don't care," Mr. Lunts replied, "but you, Chanteuse, are gonna help us clean up the place, then we're gonna have us a talk in my office."

"I'm sorry, Mr. Lunts," Chanteuse said, "but…"

"Don't be sorry, be busy," Mr. Lunts said.

"We have to move!" Vincent said, tugging Chanteuse's arm. "Forget this idiot."

"Idiot?!?" Mr. Lunts barked. "Now look, you little dweeb…"

"Mr. Lunts!" Chanteuse snapped.

"Watch that attitude, young lady," Mr. Lunts said. "Or you're gonna be in deep trouble."

"Oh, shut up," Nod said, exploding out of the root beer cup and landing a solid uppercut on Mr. Lunts's chin. The store manager flew up and backward, right into two of the approaching demons.

"There you are!" roared the third demon. "Bix has you now, pixie!"

"Heck!" cried Nod, and fled.

The demon named Bix sped after the pixie, then stopped suddenly when Vincent grabbed hold of his legs.

"Get off!" he cried, jamming its claws into Vincent's arms. Vincent yelped and let go, but Bix also yelped as magical pain jammed into him.

"I thought you said they couldn't hurt you!" Chanteuse said, seeing the blood on Vincent's arms.

"They're not allowed to," Vincent replied as he snatched a mop from a stunned employee. "That's why he's hurt, too." Vincent swung the mop around in an arc and smacked the demon right between the wings. Down Bix went, bouncing like a rubber ball when he hit the floor and landing next to an abandoned shopping cart. Vincent quickly upturned the cart, covering the demon under a mountain of milk cartons and frozen meat and vegetables and cereal boxes and cupped puddings before caging the beast with the cart's frame.

One down. But two still to go.

Those two demons crawled out from under the store manager, shook out their wings, and took to the air. Vincent charged them, swinging the mop like a pro, but the demons flew off too quickly.

"Rats!" Vincent said. "Chanteuse, we gotta…"

But Chanteuse was nowhere to be seen. Vincent grumbled, then hurried off after the demons. He hoped Nod hadn't fled the store yet, because he had another plan.

There was a loud commotion coming from several aisles away. Vincent ran, mop in hand, toward a large cloud of flour, baking soda, and pudding mix. When he arrived he saw one of the demons rubbing its eyes and flying blind. Clearly, Nod had set an effective trap. The other demon, and Nod, were gone.

"Batter up," Vincent said as the demon came within range. He swung, and hit a home run right into the demon's mouth. It chomped down even as the mop struck, biting off the end before sailing up over the aisles and away.

"Two down," Vincent said, tossing the now-useless cleaning tool and running on.

A few aisles over, Vincent picked up a spray bottle of processed cheese. That would cover the first part of his plan. Then he grabbed a can of whipped cream and a squeeze bottle of ketchup. Perfect. Now all he had to do was find Nod.

As he thought that, Nod sped past him along the floor and disappeared under the next aisle. The demon punched its way through the aisle in front of Vincent, showering him with condiment containers even as it crashed through the next aisle, chasing Nod.

Vincent took off after them, holding his items under one arm and pressing the other against his bruised chest. The pain was intense, and he didn't know how much longer he could go on.

As he passed the herbs and spices, he saw Chanteuse sitting on the floor in her meditative pose. She had taken off her work apron and had placed it on the floor in front of her, and had several tiny spice shakers all around her. As Vincent watched, she picked one up and sprinkled its contents on the apron. Vincent wanted to ask her what she was up to, but Nod needed him and so he ran on.

Man, he thought, this place is big! He was exhausting himself trying to keep up with Nod and the demon. They could fly really fast; he could not.

The store was almost devoid of people now. Many had stampeded for the exits when the demons had burst through the ceiling, and the others ran when Nod and the demon started tearing up the store. They'd made quite a mess, and the cleanup would take weeks.

Of course, they didn't have weeks. With the end of the world imminent, this store was probably closed for good.

When he arrived in the produce section, he saw Nod speed toward a melon stand and duck under it at the last second. The demon crashed into the melons, then spun around trying to dislodge a melon from his horns.

Vincent saw his chance. He ran up to the creature just as he was tossing the melon away, and sprayed him with the cheese.

"Bleagh!" the demon cried, clutching its stinging eyes. Vincent squirted it again, this time in the mouth.

"Try and taste through that stuff," Vincent said as he watched the demon gag.

That's three, Vincent thought, and he turned to find Nod.

Vincent saw Nod flying toward the bakery department. The pixie flew very slowly, nowhere near the speed he'd been at a minute ago. As Vincent caught up to him, Nod dropped down onto a loaf of freshly baked bread.

"Can't…go on," the pixie panted, unmoving. "Leave me…save yourself."

"No way," Vincent said. "I've got an idea. Hold still." He popped the top on his ketchup bottle, then pointed and squeezed.

"Hey! Mupgh…" Nod said as he was covered in condiment.

"I said hold still," Vincent said as he splattered. "This will mask your taste so they can't find you."

"Yuck," Nod said, standing and shaking some of the goop off. "Icky, but a good idea, Vincent. Thanks. What now?"

"Now we eat you!" Bix said from above.

Vincent looked up just in time to see the demon lowering an upturned shopping cart onto him. Vincent was forced to his knees and pinned, but not harmed. Bix stood on top of the cart and held it down.

"Yikes!" Nod said, and he jumped into the air. He meant to fly, but the ketchup had mucked up his wings and they didn't work the way he'd wanted. He hit the floor hard, then got to his feet and hobbled for all he was worth.

"Let me out!" Vincent cried, shaking his prison.

"I think not," Bix replied with a smug smile.

"You can't chase my friend while you're up there," Vincent told him.

"Maybe so," the demon said, "but that won't stop my friends."

Vincent looked around and saw the other two demons fly in. One still had strands of mop in its mouth, and the other was licking everything and anything to get the processed cheese off his tongue. He'd thought (hoped) they were down for the count, but demons were clearly tougher than they looked.

And they looked tough.

"That way!" said Bix, pointing in the direction the pixie had gone.

"Get off!" Vincent said, shoving at the cart Bix had dropped on him. It was useless; the demon was too strong, and Vincent had no leverage for his arms.

"Cease your struggling," Bix said. "Relax and watch as my friends devour yours."

"They'll never find him," Vincent told the demon. "I've masked his taste."

"They don't have to taste him," the demon said. "They just have to follow the ketchup."

It was true. Nod had left a trail of condiment drips an idiot could follow. Vincent shook uselessly at his metal prison, realizing not only that his friend was seconds away from being eaten but that he, Vincent, had gone and made him tastier.

The two demons followed the trail past the melon cart and around an aisle corner. Vincent stopped struggling and waited for the pixie's scream.

It didn't come. Minutes passed, and still it didn't come. Finally, the two demons re-emerged from around the aisle, looking dumbfounded.

"You lost him?" Bix asked, incredulous.

"We're sorry, Bix," one of the returning demons said. "The trail ended, and he just wasn't there. No residual taste, no nothing."

"We looked all around," the other one added. "He's just plain gone."

"Idiots!" shouted Bix. "I'll find him." He stuck out his tongue and waved it around, but after a moment or two he stopped.

"It's the ketchup," Vincent said triumphantly.

"It is not," Bix replied. "Even masked, his taste would still linger in the air. No, he has transported himself away somehow. But he can't hide forever, boy. And neither can you. You have made an enemy today, and in two days' time it will cost you dearly."

Vincent's eyes went wide and his heart and stomach clenched. Two days? That was all the time the human race had left? He hardly noticed as the demons flew away, he was so stunned. He only became aware of his surroundings again when the shopping cart suddenly lifted up and off him.

"Were ya gonna stay there forever?" Nod's voice said loud and clear, but when Vincent stood and looked around he couldn't see the pixie. Or anyone else, for that matter.

"Over here, Vincent," Chanteuse said, and then Vincent saw her holding the shopping cart. There was something funny about her. Vincent had the idea that if he took his eyes off her for a moment, she would disappear.

"It's a cloaking spell," she said. "I cast it on my apron, using herbs and spices available in the store."

"Hi, Vincent," Nod said, his hand waving from the apron's pocket. "Your friend's pretty amazing, huh?"

Vincent smiled widely. "She sure is," he said.

They heard the sounds of sirens then, and moments later several police cruisers screeched to a halt in front of the store.

"Time to go," Vincent said.

"We'll use the loading area in the back," Chanteuse said, taking his hand and leading him to the rear of the store.

• • •

An hour later, they were on a bus and halfway home. Vincent and Nod filled Chanteuse in on what was going on, and Vincent told them what the demon Bix had told him. They got some strange looks from the other passengers, but paid them no mind.

"Two days," Chanteuse said, repeating what Vincent had just told her.

"Yikes," said Nod from her apron pocket. "I knew it was coming soon, but…yikes. We've got to move fast."

"What can we do?" Vincent said. "Our only lead is Alphega Corp., and we can't get inside. They have security to keep people out, and demons to get rid of pixies."

"That means whoever is running the company knows about us," Nod said. "Wow, this is big. We've got to get in there and find out what's going on."

"We can't," Vincent said. "We'll be seen. Or tasted. There's just no way to sneak in."

"There might be a way," Chanteuse said.

"Really?" said Vincent. "What?"

"Have you ever heard," Chanteuse asked, "of astral projection?"

Vincent hadn't, so during the rest of the trip Chanteuse explained. Basically, as Vincent came to understand it, astral projection involved projecting one's soul out of one's body.

"It's what happens when we die," Chanteuse explained. "The only difference is, with astral projection you can return to your body again."

Vincent understood all about the soul. His parents had taught him that his soul would survive death, but would then be judged by the Triumvirate. He'd stand before their three massive white thrones, waiting while they reviewed his every deed and deemed them worthy or sinful. If, when all the deeds were tallied, the worthy deeds outweighed the sins, the Triumvirate would open the Book of Heaven to see if his name was written there. If it was not, he would be cast into the Flames of Eternity, otherwise known as Hell.

And if his sins outweighed the worthy deeds, there would be no need to open the Book of Heaven at all.

His parents had never explained precisely how one got one's name into the Book of Heaven. He'd asked Max about it once, and he'd said, "You just have to be Righteous enough." Like that solved anything.

"Don't worry, Vincent," Chanteuse said. "There is no judgment in the astral."

"How'd you know what I was thinking?" Vincent asked.

"I've met your parents, remember?" she replied.

"Right," Vincent said. "So you've done it, then? Astral projection?"

"I've tried," Chanteuse said.

"And?" Vincent prompted when Chanteuse didn't elaborate. "Have you actually done it?"

"Yes, Vincent," she said. "I have."

"That's great!" said Nod. "She can project and go to Alphega for us."

"No, I can't," Chanteuse said.

"What d'you mean, you can't?" Nod asked. "You said you could do it, so what's the problem?"

"Nod, shut up," Vincent said. Chanteuse's usual cheerful smile had disappeared and her face had darkened.

She hadn't had that look since the day Vincent's parents had fired her, and it broke Vincent's heart to see it.

"What is it?" he asked gently, taking Chanteuse's hand. It seemed the right thing to do, and she didn't object.

"The last time I projected," Chanteuse replied, "I met a spirit who gave me a warning. He told me the next time I projected, someone I love dearly would die."

"What?" said Nod. "The jerk!"

"It wasn't a threat," Chanteuse said. "More a prediction of the future. The next time I project, something bad will happen, an accident perhaps. And I'm scared it will be my mother."

"That settles it, then," Vincent said. "You don't have to do it." He squeezed her hand reassuringly, and she gave him a smile. Wow, he thought. I'm holding Chanteuse's hand. And she's smiling at me!

"We don't want anything to happen to your mom," he told her. "Do we?" he stared hard at Nod, who shrank back into his pocket.

"Hey, 'course not," Nod said. "But someone here has to project, and it can't be me. Those demons can taste your soul as easily as they can taste your body."

"Really?" Vincent asked.

"That's what I heard," Nod said. "I'm not about to chance it. Would you?"

Vincent, remembering the demons' tooth-filled mouths, didn't think he would.

"That leaves me," Vincent said.

The bus arrived at Chanteuse's stop, so she stood and rang the bell. They got off, ignoring the laughter and shouts of, "Freaks!" and hurried toward her house.

"Can you teach me?" Vincent asked Chanteuse as they walked. They were still holding hands, and his spirits were soaring.

"I will try," she replied. "But it isn't easy, Vincent. To be successful, you'll have to focus, ignore all distractions…Vincent, are you listening?"

Vincent wasn't listening. He stared straight ahead, and gulped.

"There you are," said Max, hands on hips and frown full of menace. "You are in big trouble, little brother."

"Mother and Father are furious," Max said, stomping toward Vincent and Chanteuse. "And they don't even know the full truth! I followed you this morning, Vincent. I saw the creature you consorted with. No doubt the same creature that attacked me in the Chapel last night!"

"Max," Vincent said as calmly as he could, "this really isn't a good time."

"And now," Max continued, "I find you hand-in-hand with the witch."

Vincent fought the fear to let go of Chanteuse. He had every right to hold her hand, regardless of what his family thought. Besides, he really didn't want to let go.

"Mother and Father waited an hour for you at the school," Max went on. "The principal is furious. And Big Tom's parents were mortified."

A deluge of guilt choked Vincent. He'd forgotten about his forced fight with his best friend.

"Is he okay?" Vincent croaked.

"As if you'd care!" his brother snapped.

"Has something happened to Big Tom?" Chanteuse asked.

"Be silent, witch!" Max said, whipping out a pocket Text of the Triumvirate and holding it before him like a shield.

"Hey!" said Nod, poking his head out of the apron pocket. "You can't talk to her like that."

"Aagh!" Max cried, stepping back. "Another demon!"

"Nod, stay down," Vincent said, pushing the pixie back in. "You don't want the demons to find you." He turned quickly back to his brother and said, "Calm down, Max. It's not what you think. In fact, it's worse."

"You've got that right."

Vincent groaned as he turned and saw Grimbowl standing by the side of Chanteuse's home. This was all he needed.

"Stay back!" Max said, swiveling around and pointing his Text at the elf. "In the name of the Triumvirate, I command thee to…"

"Shut up," Grimbowl said. "Vincent, smack him."

Vincent was only too happy to oblige. Max took a full step back, raised a hand to his cheek, and stared at his brother in astonished outrage.

"Vincent!" said Chanteuse, who was similarly surprised.

"Sorry, Max," said Vincent, who was also amazed he'd actually done it. He'd had no choice; the obyon would have agonized him if he'd refused, but Max was his brother and he'd hit him.

And Big Tom was his best friend, but he'd hit him, too. What other horrible things would the elves force him to do?

"So this is your choice," Max said, staring hard at his little brother. "You would rather ally yourself with these foul things than with your family? And what of your commitment to the Triumvirate?"

"Bo-ring!" Grimbowl said. "Vincent, smack him again. Harder."

"No," said Vincent. The moment the words left his lips, the pain stabbed right through his head. Vincent clenched his teeth and clapped his hands around his temples, but the pain got worse.

"Vincent?" Chanteuse said, but he could hardly hear her.

"Brother?" Max asked, and there was genuine concern in his voice.

"Aaagh!" Vincent cried, and slapped Max. Harder.

"Good," said Grimbowl. "Now reach into Chanteuse's pocket and squish that pixie."

"What?" said Nod, poking his head out again.

"No!" said Chanteuse, throwing her hands over her apron pocket.

"No!" shouted Vincent. The agony was tremendous, but he did not—would not—move. If he didn't draw the line now, he would become a murderer.

But the pain was overwhelming. It was too much. He fell to his knees, screaming and clawing at his skull.

He wondered if he was going to die, and then he hoped he would. Anything for relief from the pain.

Anything except murder.

Someone grabbed him by the back of his shirt and hauled him to his feet. He was pulled forward, stumbling along on legs he could hardly feel toward a destination he couldn't see because his eyes were shut tight. He remembered his parents telling him of the Soul Harvester, a fallen angel who would drag the unrighteous to face the Triumvirate on their white thrones at the moment of death. Was that happening to him now?

The pain became so great that Vincent could no longer think. He let his captor take him where they would, and hoped it would all be over soon.

And then it was.

Vincent blinked, felt his head. The pain was gone. Completely.

It was replaced by a severe tickling in his nostrils. He sneezed, then sneezed again. When he sneezed for the third time, a bug flew out of his nose.

Vincent stared down at the ladybug, and realization dawned. That bug had been the obyon. Now that it was out of him, he was free.

"I'm free!" he cried, looking up. He was inside

Chanteuse's house, just beyond the front door. Chanteuse stood beside him; it had been her who had grabbed him, not the Soul Harvester.

Grimbowl stood in the doorway, looking most displeased. Max ran up the front steps behind him, looking confused.

"What in Creation is going on here?" he asked.

"I'll explain later, Max," Vincent said, then he looked up at Chanteuse. "What did you do?"

"I brought you inside," she replied. "My house is protected by magical wards. Any magic items that enter here are instantly rendered useless."

"Hah!" Vincent said, smirking smugly at Grimbowl. He saw the ladybug skittering away and wanted to squash it, but before he could Chanteuse snatched it up off the floor.

"What is this?" she asked the elf.

"A bug?" Grimbowl said innocently.

"It is a lot more than that, elf," Nod said from the apron pocket.

"Tell her," Vincent said. "Tell her what you and your friends did to me."

Grimbowl opened his mouth as if to speak, then he

charged forward. He tried to get out through the front door, but Max had that exit blocked.

"There is no escape for you, evil one," Max said, thrusting forward his Text.

"Oh yes there is," Grimbowl said, turning and running the other way. He zipped past Vincent and Chanteuse and nearly made it to the backdoor.

"Aagh!" Grimbowl cried as a large hand clamped around his waist.

"Where do you think you're going?" Miss Sloam said, holding the elf triumphantly.

"Tell me," Chanteuse said, holding out the insect. "What is this thing?"

"It's an obyon," Grimbowl said, and he told her what an obyon was. Chanteuse listened with growing horror, and when the elf finished she was in a full-blown rage.

"How could you!" she shouted at the elf. "How could you do that to my friend? You little monster!"

"You used your wicked sorcery to command my brother," Max said. "There is no mercy in Heaven for a wretch like you."

"I would rather you had done that to me," Chanteuse continued, "than to one of my friends."

"I couldn't do that!" Grimbowl said. "You're...well, you're the one person we elves can trust. And you treat us like we're good."

"I was clearly wrong about that," Chanteuse said.

Grimbowl reacted as if slapped. Tears formed in his eyes, and for a moment Vincent actually felt sorry for him. It seemed the elf was more dependent on Chanteuse's good graces than he'd let on.

Not that Vincent could blame him. He knew he'd be devastated if Chanteuse called him a bad person. She was like that. You couldn't stand for her to not like you.

"What shall we do with him?" Chanteuse's mother asked.

"Burn him," Max said. "Then burn that little one in the apron. And as for the witch..."

"Max, not now," Vincent said, standing back up. "There's a lot here you don't understand."

"And I'm not waiting around for him to figure it out," Grimbowl said, and then his whole body went limp.

"What happened to him?" Vincent asked, walking over to Chanteuse's mom.

"Don't know," said Miss Sloam, giving the elf a shake. "Looks dead. Didn't think I squeezed him that hard."

Vincent reached out and poked Grimbowl's stomach. Nothing happened. He flicked one of the elf's legs. It swayed like a branch in the wind, but nothing more.

"Check his breathing," Nod said. "Bet you anything he's faking it."

Vincent licked his finger and held it in front of Grimbowl's nose. He felt air on his finger, and then he felt teeth.

"Ow!" he cried, yanking his finger out of Grimbowl's mouth.

"You are all in big trouble now," the elf said. "I just went and got help. My entire tribe will be here in five minutes to rescue me."

"You didn't go anywhere," Vincent pointed out as he rubbed his finger. "You've been right here the whole time."

"Ever hear of astral projection?" Grimbowl said. "We elves are experts."

"Really?" Vincent said, raising an eyebrow.

"Is that so?" Nod said as he climbed out of the pocket. "Well, when I'm done with you, your astral body'll be all that's left of…"

"Nod! Stay in my pocket," Chanteuse said, grabbing

him and pushing him back. "You won't be cloaked if you come out."

"Cloaked from what?" Grimbowl asked.

"None of your business," Vincent shot back.

"Because if that's a magical cloak," Grimbowl went on, "then it won't work in a ward-protected house, will it?"

Vincent, Chanteuse, and Nod stared at the elf and said, "What?"

Then Vincent and Chanteuse looked at each other, then down at Nod.

"Oh, no," the pixie said.

"So what was it supposed to cloak him from?" Grimbowl asked.

A moment later, he found out.

With a loud crash, the three demons burst through the living room window into Chanteuse's house. Bix led them, and he looked very pleased.

"Well, well, what a feast we have here!" he said, looking from Nod to Grimbowl.

"Ulp," said Nod.

"Demons!" screamed Grimbowl. "Letmegoletme-goletmego!"

"Demons?" said Max. "But all of you are…"

"Not now, Max," Vincent said.

Miss Sloam dropped the elf and sized up the new intruders. Vincent guessed that she, like her daughter, had seen a lot of strange creatures in her time. Judging from the look on her face, however, these winged, round monsters were something new.

"Get out of my house," she said.

The demons ignored her and charged. Two of them made a beeline for Nod, who scrambled out of Chanteuse's apron and took flight. The third demon veered off and followed the fleeing Grimbowl.

Chanteuse's mother swung a fist and pounded the demon full in the face. Vincent kicked up with his left leg and nailed Bix under the chin. The last demon pushed past Max and lunged at Nod.

"Stop!" Chanteuse cried, throwing herself in its path. The demon shoved her aside, scratching her with its claws as it did so. Chanteuse yelped and fell back, blood seeping from cuts on her arm and shoulder.

"What the…" the demon said, looking from its claws to Chanteuse's wounds.

"What the…" Vincent said as he stood up. "Shouldn't you be howling in pain?"

Bix, who had bounced off the ceiling, took in the situation and smiled.

"My magic wards…" Chanteuse said.

Vincent felt a sick feeling of doom. He looked at Bix, and realized the demon knew it, too.

"Open season, boys!" Bix said, and charged. He slammed into Vincent's chest, knocking him backward into the kitchen.

Vincent gasped, out of breath and drowning in pain. His chest had just started to heal, but now it felt like he'd been smashed open. He lay helplessly on the kitchen floor as Bix exposed his teeth and dropped onto him.

"No!" cried Max, leaping forward and knocking the demon away. He landed squarely on his brother's chest, and Vincent wished he could die right then.

Chanteuse screamed. Max and Vincent looked up and saw her mother grabbing hold of one demon while holding another under her foot.

"Those are demons?" Max asked as he climbed off his brother.

"Uuugh…" Vincent replied.

"Then what are the others?" Max asked.

"Uunng…" Vincent replied.

Bix recovered and charged again. Max grabbed a chair and held it up, but the demon tore through it like a bullet through a wet napkin. Max backed away, trod on Vincent's chest, and fell backward. Vincent moaned and wished the demons would finish him off quickly. Bix hovered over him, mouth open wide, prepared to grant that wish.

Max lashed out with both legs, meaning to send the beast flying. His aim was a little off, however, and only his left foot struck the demon. His right foot, unfortunately, connected solidly with Vincent's jaw. The room swam out of focus, and then everything went black.

• • •

Vincent awoke in a white room. His jaw and chest hurt a lot, but he was lying down on something comfortable. He tried to sit up, but then the pain in his chest got much worse.

"Ow," he said, but he tried again. His last memory hadn't been a good one, and he needed to know where he was. Using his arms instead of his chest muscles, Vincent raised himself up and looked around.

He was in a hospital room. There were two beds

in the room, and his brother sat upon the other. Their parents stood on either side of Max, hands on his shoulders and concern on their faces. A tall man in a white coat stood on the other side of the bed, and when he saw Vincent he smiled and walked over.

"Good evening," the tall man said. "I am Doctor Ritchet. How are you feeling?"

"You have some explaining to do, young man," his father said, shoving Doctor Ritchet aside and glaring down at him. "First of all…"

"We were so worried!" his mother cut in. "Are you all right, Vincent?"

"I'm…" Vincent began.

"He's clearly all right," his father said. "Now that he's awake, I think he should answer a few questions, such as where he's been all afternoon."

Vincent's mother looked conflicted. Vincent suspected she agreed with his father, but she clearly hadn't forgotten her encounter with the "angel," either.

"Your son needs to rest," Doctor Ritchet said. "And I'll need to keep both boys here overnight for observation."

"What?" said Vincent's dad. "But there's nothing wrong with them."

"Yes there is," Vincent said, touching his jaw.

"Your sons have numerous cuts and bruises," the doctor said. "It is not yet safe to discharge them."

"Because of cuts and bruises?" Vincent's father said. "In my day, they'd already be at home, getting thrashed for missing school!"

"That's not how things are done now," Doctor Ritchet said firmly. "Now I must ask you to leave."

"Let's go, Gerald," Mrs. Drear said, taking his arm.

"They had better be out in time for Friday's protest," Mr. Drear said, allowing himself to be led.

"You will be notified as soon as your boys are fit to be discharged," the doctor told him. "This way."

Vincent watched as Doctor Ritchet escorted his parents out. He was too tired to be angry with them. They would remain the same until the end of the world. Or two days' time. Whichever came first.

"Max?" Vincent said, turning to look at his brother. "Max, what happened?"

Max looked away, and Vincent thought he was angry. When he turned back, however, there were tears in his eyes.

"I thought I knew everything," Max said. "I have Sinned, Vincent. I have been arrogant."

Vincent would have agreed with him, but suspected now was the wrong time. His brother had stood with him, and saved his life from the demon attack.

"Don't be hard on yourself," he said. "You did good."

He wanted to say more, but time was short. He felt so very sleepy, and he needed information before he nodded off.

"What happened at the house?" he asked. "Is Chanteuse okay?"

Max paused, then looked his little brother in the eyes.

"No, she is not," he said. "She and her mother were hurt badly by the demons. They would have been killed, but then your tiny friend returned."

"Nod?" Vincent asked.

"I do not know his name," Max said. "He was the one in the witch's apron pocket."

"That's him," Vincent said, struggling to sit up again. "What happened to him?"

"He attacked the demons," Max said. "It was the bravest thing I have ever seen. The little thing was clearly no match for the three beasts, but still he fought them. And when all three were fighting him, he flew off and the demons followed. He saved all our lives, Vincent. I had thought such creatures were servants of the Devil, but the Triumvirate have opened my eyes."

"Glad to hear it," Vincent said. His head was very dizzy now, and he could not stay awake much longer. "Max, I need your help. I need you to find Grimbowl, that elf who ran away from Chanteuse's house."

"The one who had you in thrall?" Max said. "No, Vincent. That creature is evil."

"I need him," Vincent said. "Chanteuse was going to help me to do an astral projection so I could sneak into Alphega's headquarters, but she can't help me now. Grimbowl said he was an expert…"

"No, Vincent," Max said. "Such things are unnatural."

"Max…" Vincent said. He needed to reach his brother, but how?

"Max," he said, "do you really think I'm asking you to do evil? Don't think, just answer."

"I…no, Vincent. But the Triumvirate…"

"I need Grimbowl," Vincent said. He fell back onto his bed, exhaustion claiming him. "I have to…you must…"

And then he was asleep.

• • •

Vincent dreamed. It was one of those dreams that makes perfect sense while you're in it, but none at all the moment you wake up. He stood upon a raft on a fast-moving river, heading straight for a waterfall. He held a hoop in his hands, and was trying to convince the cows swimming in the river below to jump through it.

He was not alone on the raft. Two trees grew out of the raft on either side of him, and they swished their branches at Vincent and tried to make him put the hoop down. Vincent explained to the trees that the cows had to jump through the hoop before they reached the waterfall, but naturally the trees weren't listening.

Vincent felt very frustrated—couldn't the trees see the waterfall? They would if they just looked. Instead the trees told him the cows needed to spin in the water. If they did so, they would be saved from certain doom when the train came. There is no train, Vincent argued, but the trees assured him a train was indeed coming, and would run through the river at any moment. All the cows who were not spinning, the trees explained, would surely perish.

So it went, with Vincent's raft sailing down cow-infested waters while he tried to keep the trees from taking his hoop. And it might have gotten stranger than that, but just then another figure appeared on the raft.

"Nice dream," said Grimbowl. "Like the symbolism. Good touch."

"Grimbowl," Vincent said, distantly remembering he needed the elf's help. "Can you help me? We have to get these cows to…"

"No we don't," Grimbowl said. "You're in a dream, and I'm going to pull you out of it."

"Dream?" Vincent said. "But the cows…" He waved the hoop, as if in explanation.

"All symbols, kid," the elf said. "The river is the world, the waterfall the end of it. The cows are the people, and this hoop," he took the object from Vincent's hands, "is you trying to save them. Easy. And the trees are your parents. That one's pretty obvious. Get it?"

Vincent looked around and saw his dream with a more objective eye. Now that the elf had drawn attention to it, the whole thing did seem a bit silly. Symbolic, yes, but silly. And why cows? What was that all about?

"Okay, so it's a dream," Vincent said. "Should I wake up now?"

"No, don't do that," Grimbowl said. "Just take my hand and come with me."

He held up his hand, and Vincent reached for it.

"You're not going to stick anything up my nose, are you?" Vincent asked.

"No," Grimbowl replied, and he pulled Vincent off the raft and out of his dream.

Vincent and Grimbowl floated in the air in a dark room. There was something very familiar about it, and when he looked around Vincent saw why.

"This is my hospital room," he said. He could see the door on one side, the window on the other. He saw Max standing beside his bed, holding Grimbowl in his arms. A needle-thin cord stretched from the elf's head all the way to the Grimbowl who floated in the air beside Vincent.

"What the…?" Vincent said, looking from one Grimbowl to the other. "How can you be in two places at once?"

"I'm not the only one," Grimbowl said, pointing down.

Vincent looked. Below was his bed, and lying in that bed…

"Woah!" Vincent said, recoiling at the sight of his own face.

"Don't get scared, calm down," Grimbowl said. "Strong emotions will snap you right back to your body."

"What? I don't…" Vincent said, but then he understood. "I'm having an astral projection, aren't I?"

"What was your first clue?" said Grimbowl.

"I thought it would be really hard to do," Vincent said, looking down at his sleeping form. Like Grimbowl, he had a thin silver cord stretching out of his forehead into the back of his astral skull. Vincent reached back and felt it; it was like having a tail in the base of his neck.

"It usually is hard," Grimbowl said. "A lot of concentration and focus. But everyone leaves their bodies when they dream, kid. They hover above their bodies and surround themselves in their own personal dreamworlds. If you know the trick, you can pull someone out of their dream.

"But enough about that. Your brother said you needed me to help you do this. What I want to know is, why?"

"My brother?" Vincent looked back at Max, now sitting on the bed with Grimbowl's body still in his arms. "He actually found you?"

"Wasn't hard," Grimbowl said. "I was here anyway. I wanted to ask you what you're up to, hanging around with pixies and fighting demons."

"I shouldn't tell you," Vincent said, turning away from him. "You made me beat up my best friend. And you hurt me. A lot."

"I did what I had to," Grimbowl said. "We needed a human to go where we couldn't."

"You should have just asked," Vincent said. "That's what Nod did."

"Good for him," Grimbowl said. "He's one terrific pixie, that's for sure."

"I thought you elves hated pixies," Vincent asked.

"We do, yeah," Grimbowl said. "My people, Vincent, we're not exactly big on trust for other species. Goes all the way back to our epoch, when the Centaurs..."

"I know," Vincent said. "Nod told me about them."

"Did he?" Grimbowl said. "What else do you know?"

"I know we have less than two days until the end of the epoch," Vincent said.

"What?" Grimbowl replied.

"So we don't really have time for your trust issues," Vincent pointed out. "We need to get on with this before we lose any more time."

"You know what, kid?" Grimbowl said. "You're right. And I was wrong about you. You're not just some dolt."

"Wow, thanks," Vincent said dryly.

"I can do better," the elf said. "We shouldn't have stuck that obyon in you. You're a good kid. And we might just owe all our lives to you."

Vincent smiled at that. "Thank you," he said.

"Okay, enough mushy stuff. If we've only got two days, then we've got to move."

Grimbowl grabbed Vincent's hand, and the world around them blurred. Before Vincent could ask what was going on, they appeared in the middle of a street.

A truck came right at them, and roared through their astral bodies before Vincent had a chance to scream.

"Relax, kid," Grimbowl said. "We're in the astral. Physical stuff can't hurt us."

"You could have warned me," Vincent said.

"Yeah," Grimbowl replied, "but this way was funnier."

Vincent shot him a dirty look, then turned and took in their surroundings.

They were in the suburbs, right in front of an expensive-looking two-level house. All the houses on the street looked expensive—this must be the rich part of town, Vincent thought. And there's only one person he knew who lived in this area.

"We're outside Barnaby Wilkins's house," Grimbowl said. "You're going in there."

"Why?"

"So you can look through his stuff," Grimbowl said. "Maybe he left his science fair project out where you can read it."

"No," Vincent said. "I don't need to look at his stuff. Nod and I found a better place to look for Portal Sites."

"Where?" Grimbowl asked.

"Alphega Corporate Headquarters," Vincent replied.

"Then why are we still here?" Grimbowl said, grabbing Vincent's astral hand again. "Lead the way!"

"Okay," Vincent said. "How, exactly?"

"Oh yeah, you're new at this," Grimbowl said. "We could fly there, but thought travel is even faster. That's how we got here, kid. Easy to learn, too. If you know where you want to go, think hard about being there and it'll happen."

"Okay," Vincent said, closing his eyes and thinking. It was hard at first, because his mind kept drifting to other things. For example, if he wasn't in his body, how could he close his eyes? Did he even have eyes? Or hands? How was he holding Grimbowl's hand if he wasn't in a physical body?

"Focus more," Grimbowl said, kicking Vincent in the astral shins.

Vincent focused, and a moment later they were at the edge of Alphega Corp.'s parking lot. The towering headquarters stood before them, and to Vincent's astral eyes there was something different about it. Translucent spheres surrounded the structure, giving it a slight fishbowl appearance. It reminded Vincent of the shields that protected spaceships in science fiction shows like *Infinite Destiny*, and when he mentioned this to Grimbowl he found he was not wrong.

"Looks like magical wards," the elf said. "Could be to shield them from magical attacks. Or it could be to detect astral travelers, but I don't think that's possible. Either way, it's one heck of a security system."

"Yeah," Vincent said. "And they've got demons, too."

"What?" Grimbowl said. "Demons? Here?"

"Yeah," Vincent said. "I think they're patrolling the area. That's why…"

"You didn't tell me there were demons!" Grimbowl said, starting to panic. His silver cord, which had been trailing loosely behind him, started to tighten. "Kid, they can taste everything, even souls! If they detect my spirit, they'll trace me back to my…"

He never finished, because his silver cord pulled taut and yanked his soul away.

At first Vincent worried that a demon had somehow caught him. Then he remembered what the elf had said about strong emotions. Grimbowl had been pulled back to his body.

"I guess I'm on my own," Vincent said, turning

back to the building. It would be risky; if the wards could detect astral travelers, they would know he was there before he got to the front door. If they found him, could they do anything to him? Was it possible to hurt a soul? The idea alone was just plain scary.

But if the Portal Site was here, the world needed to know. Max, Chanteuse, and her mother had all been hurt trying to help him, and Nod had given his life. Could he do any less?

Vincent walked forward until he was right in front of the ward. This was it, the moment of truth.

"Oh boy," he said, and stepped through it.

Sirens, claxons, and alarms did not go off, and an army of demons did not materialize and start chasing him. Vincent waited a minute, then two. Nothing. He seemed to be in the clear.

"I seem to be in the clear," he said, then covered his astral mouth. The last thing he needed was to jinx himself.

Still nothing happened. Vincent waited a few more moments, just to be safe, then he ventured forward once more. He thought about the front doors, and a split second later he was there. He waved his astral hands in front of the security guards, but they didn't notice.

"So far, so good," Vincent said, watching the guards for a reaction. There was none; they could neither see nor hear him.

"Right," said Vincent. "This is it."

Vincent walked past the guards, and entered Alphega Corporate Headquarters.

The building was bustling with activity, which Vincent found surprising. It was still late at night, after all, and a normal company would have been closed.

He stood in a small lobby, with several corridors branching off in all directions. Employees moved this way and that, carrying important-looking documents, all looking stressed out of their minds.

One corridor led to the elevators. Beside it, Vincent found the building's directory. He looked it over, hoping for some clue, like a sign saying, "this way to the portal," but nothing sprang out at him.

Vincent followed one of the other corridors, and found himself in an office. It was long but not wide, L-shaped, and filled to capacity with row upon row of cubicles. Employees sat in those cubicles, typing feverishly at their computer terminals. Each terminal had an extra monitor attached, exactly like the ones on the superstore cash registers.

Other employees rushed this way and that with their documents. One person rushed straight through Vincent, and she let off a yelp of surprise. She looked around, trying to determine what had happened, but she couldn't see Vincent. Puzzled, she walked on.

Vincent also had a bit of a shock, having just been walked through. He recovered just in time to see another employee walking straight at him, but not in time to get out of the way.

"Yaah!" the man said, having an involuntary shiver.

"Interesting," Vincent said, watching the man walk

away. It seemed people could feel his presence when they passed through him.

He would have liked to explore this new knowledge more fully, but something turned the corner up ahead and grabbed Vincent's attention. It was a demon, lazily floating a meter above the heads of the employees. The people didn't react to its presence, but the demon watched them very closely. It carried a small device in its hand, but it was too far away for Vincent to see what it was.

Vincent rushed into an empty cubicle and ducked down. He didn't think the demon would be able to see him, but he couldn't afford to take the chance. He stayed as low as he could while still high enough to keep an eye on the creature.

The demon paused in the air over an employee who had stopped working to yawn. The demon tapped something into its handheld device, and suddenly that employee's second monitor sprang to life.

"Milton Judge," said the digitized face of Mr. Wilkins, "you have been found engaging in activities not associated with company policy. A one-hour pay cut will be applied to your account."

Oh man, Vincent thought. Whoever runs Alphega really hates their employees.

The demon drifted off again, moving closer. Vincent ducked down farther, and leaned on the desk for support...

...and fell through it. He didn't hit the floor, but he stopped falling just above it. The desk was all around and above him, and when he stood back up his head emerged from the desktop like a ghost. Which, he supposed, he was.

Vincent crouched down, and the desk enveloped him again. This, he thought, was cool. He was a ghost! He could walk through stuff! Except, it seemed, the floor. Why was that? It was no more solid than the desk. How had he been walking on it?

Vincent reached down, and his hand went through the floor. Now what? He was still crouching on the floor, and yet he could put his hand through it. Maybe...

Maybe it was in his mind. Maybe the floor was solid beneath him so long as he wanted it that way...

This was fascinating, absolutely, but he still had a job to do. Vincent stood back up, and that's when he remembered why he'd ducked down in the first place. He looked around and saw the demon, now much closer. It hadn't noticed him, much to Vincent's relief.

He stayed still as the demon passed by, then he backed away slowly…

…into the next cubicle, where a man was working hard at his computer. Vincent walked backward through that computer, and it sparked and shut down with a bang.

"Woah!" the man cried, falling backward off his chair.

The demon stopped and turned, and stared intently at the smoking computer. Vincent backed away once more, only to run afoul of the man's printer.

"Yikes!" the man cried as his printer sparked and shorted out. Heads popped up from cubicles, and a crowd began to gather. The demon eyed the area suspiciously, then it stuck out its tongue and tasted the air.

Time to go, Vincent thought, and he turned and ran. Right through another computer. Then he went through a photocopier and a fax machine. All three machines shorted out with a shower of sparks, and the paper trap in the copier caught fire. The fire alarm sounded a few seconds later.

Souls and electronics don't mix, Vincent realized as he ran. He ducked around the L-shaped corner, and came upon another office full of cubicles. All around him, people left their desks and headed for the exits. A few went through Vincent, and yelped as they did so. Vincent tried to get out of their way, only to run into more electronic machines.

"Not good," he said as he shorted another computer. The demon drifted toward him, its tongue swishing from side to side. Vincent envied the demon, being able to fly above the throng of employees unnoticed.

Then he remembered something Grimbowl had said. When Vincent had asked how they would get to Alphega Corp., the elf had told him they could fly. That would mean that Vincent, in his astral body, could fly!

But how? Vincent thought about it, and wondered if it would work the same way as the thought-travel. He pictured himself lifting off and hovering over the cubicles…

…and it happened. Vincent floated into the air, and before he could stop himself he went through the ceiling and into the second floor. He came up in the middle of another computer, shorting it out and giving the nearby evacuating employees a start. Vincent continued his ascent, and made it up to the seventh floor before he thought about stopping. When he did so, his upward travel ceased.

"Neat," Vincent said, his mind awash with the possibilities. However, he still had a portal to find. He imagined himself flying around the office, and off he went.

Five minutes later, he'd done a complete orbit of the seventh floor. He'd seen and hid from another demon, but otherwise there was nothing out of the ordinary. He dropped down to the sixth floor and checked it out, then he tried the fifth. Each floor had a demon patrolling it, but otherwise there was nothing strange or supernatural.

However, something nagged at Vincent, and it came to him as he flew around the fourth floor. The offices were very long but not wide. It was as if a huge chunk of the building was missing. And it was missing from the building's center.

Vincent turned and faced the wall. Something was hidden beyond it, and he meant to find out what it was.

He was about to fly toward and through the wall when he was distracted by a demon's tongue. It slashed right through his astral form, then slashed back and stopped in the middle of Vincent's torso.

Vincent spun around and looked at the demon that hovered just behind him. There was something familiar about this demon; Vincent had seen him once before. It wasn't one of the three that had chased and killed Nod. Rather, it was Rennik, the one who had tasted him in the parking lot.

"Ah ha!" Rennik said, grinning an evil grin. "There you are."

Vincent felt a ball of fear growing in his astral guts, and he backed off. His silver cord started to tighten, and he forced himself to calm down. He'd come too far to be whisked back to his body now. And so what if the demon knew he was there? He couldn't touch him or hurt him in any way.

And, the demon couldn't go through walls.

"Bye, bye," Vincent said and he turned and leapt through the wall. For a second he could hear Rennik's angry scream, then there was silence. The wall was thick; Vincent flew for a full second before emerging on the other side.

He found himself in another office. It was twice as large as his bedroom, and lushly furnished. A shiny hand-carved oak desk sat upon a brilliant green carpet, facing a large picture window. Paintings hung on the walls, some depicting fantasy creatures and others showing wild horses. The picture window's shades were drawn, but Vincent could see a brilliant illumination around them. There was a very bright light on the other side, and Vincent wondered what it was. It couldn't have been the sun; the office was in the middle of a building, and anyway, it was still nighttime.

A man sat at the desk in a chair that was also handcrafted from the finest wood. The man sat up straight, wore an expensive-looking brown suit, and appeared absorbed in a video conference call. He hadn't noticed Vincent, and Vincent hoped it would stay that way.

"Yes, I'm aware it violates international law," the man said to a Chinese man whose face was displayed in a video monitor. "That's never stopped us before, has it? I don't care if UN inspectors are coming by. Just keep the workers in the factory. I tell you what, in two days time you can let them have a day off, all right? Good."

He punched a button, and the Chinese man vanished from the screen.

Beside the desk, Vincent saw something rather strange. It looked like a metal box on two long metal legs, with lots of electronic connectors within it. Vincent would have given it a closer look, but he was distracted by the hay.

The desk had three drawers, and the middle one was open and full of hay. Vincent thought that was kind of strange, but not nearly as strange as what he saw next. The man lazily reached a hand into the drawer, grabbed a fistful of hay, and started snacking.

"He...eats hay," Vincent said, watching with puzzled fascination. "O-kay."

Just then there was a knock at the door. The man slammed his drawer shut, wiped the hay crumbs from the front of his suit, and said, "Enter."

Vincent turned to see who was coming in. For a moment he feared it would be Rennik, but it was not. Instead, it was Mr. Wilkins.

"Ah, Francis," the man said. "I was just dealing with our friends in China, a task I believe I'd assigned to you."

"Indeed you did, Mr. Edwards," Wilkins said. "However, in this instance..."

"Have you forgotten our arrangement?" Mr. Edwards went on. "I would hate to have to take back my part of it."

"I have not forgotten, Mr. Edwards," Wilkins said.

Take that, Vincent thought with an astral smirk.

"See that you do not," Mr. Edwards said. "Have they identified the cause of the fire alarm?"

"Yes, Mr. Edwards," Wilkins replied. "It seems an astral traveler has infiltrated the building."

"Post-epochal?" Mr. Edwards asked.

"No, sir," said Wilkins. "The demons say it is a human."

Woah, Vincent thought. Barnaby's dad knows about demons.

"Nay," Mr. Edwards said. "This complicates matters. Who is it?"

"They don't know yet, sir," Wilkins said. "It may just be a random traveler, a human who has no idea what he is…"

"Even if that is the case," Mr. Edwards snapped, "he will still see things that he must not. We are close, Francis, very close. And I will nay have a human, especially not one capable of astral travel, spreading the word. I must speak with the others. Bring me to my legs."

Wilkins walked around Mr. Edwards and lifted him out of his chair. Vincent let off an astral gasp; the man had no legs. Wilkins carried Mr. Edwards over to the metal box beside the desk, and set him down into it. Vincent understood then; the box was a metal waist, atop robotic legs.

"Come, Francis," Mr. Edwards said, walking to the door. His legs made a slight electrical shifting sound, and the footfalls were loud.

"Sir," Wilkins said before they got to the door, "with

the end of the epoch so close at hand, and given what is coming, is it not time to have my son brought here?"

Edwards stopped, turned to him.

"Nay, Francis," Edwards said. "There are appearances to consider."

"I hardly think the disappearance of one boy will be noticed," Wilkins said.

"Then you are a fool," Edwards replied. "He is being watched, Francis. Possibly by the same being making his astral intrusion into this building now. If Barnaby were to be plucked from his normal routine, it would send a clear message to his watchers that something is going on. Nay, Barnaby stays where he is. For now."

"Yes, sir," Wilkins said, clearly unhappy but just as clearly beaten.

Just then, Rennik flew in with his tongue fully extended.

"Rennik!" said Mr. Edwards, stepping back to avoid a tongue-lashing. "What is the meaning of this intrusion?"

"He's here," Rennik explained. "The invading entity is here, I can taste him!"

Vincent was already moving. He sped out of the office, straight through the picture window…

It was beautiful. Tall, arch-shaped and radiating light, Vincent had no doubt at all that this was the portal site. It dazzled; the portal itself looked like it was made up of millions of glowing crystals. It called to him, inviting him to enter.

The guards on either side of the portal were not so inviting. Several demons patrolled around it, and a couple of men as big as Barnaby Wilkins's bodyguards stood in front, holding machine guns. There was no way anyone would be sneaking past them. Not that they'll even know the portal is here, Vincent thought. The building covered the portal completely, hiding it from view.

Vincent heard a smash from behind him. He turned and saw Rennik hovering in the broken picture window, staring right at him.

"You can't escape me," the demon said. "I can taste you. I'll find you, no matter where you hide."

"Stand down, Rennik," Mr. Edwards said, arriving at the broken window beside him. "I cannot see you, whoever you are, but I know you are there."

He's talking to me, Vincent thought, feeling another knot of fear inside him. The guy who's hiding the Portal Sites is talking to me!

"Listen well," Edwards went on, staring straight

through Vincent. "You have seen too much. I will find you, and I shall silence you."

Vincent's silver cord tightened, and this time he did not resist. His cord pulled taut, and propelled Vincent's astral form back to his body.

Vincent awoke with a start. It was that fast. He had no memory at all of traveling across the city and back to the hospital; it had just happened.

Already Vincent missed the many advantages of his spirit form. For one, his astral body didn't feel pain.

His chest and jaw still hurt, but not nearly as much as before. He would probably be going home today.

Vincent forced himself upward into a sitting position and looked around. He was bursting to tell someone what he'd found out, but there was no one. Max was sound asleep in his bed, and Grimbowl simply wasn't there. Why had the elf left? What could've been more important to him than the information Vincent now possessed?

Vincent lay back down again. There was nothing he could do until the elves contacted him. He could wake his brother and tell him, but Max had been through a lot and deserved his sleep. After all, it was the second-to-last sleep he would ever have...

Vincent sat back up again, faster this time. The world had less than two days, maybe only one day left now. The demon Bix had told Vincent the news yesterday in the grocery store, at around four in the afternoon. Was yesterday one of the two days? Or was it two days plus yesterday? When had the two-day countdown actually started?

Vincent got out of bed. He was too restless to sleep, and there was so little time left. He walked over to Max's bed and shook his brother by the shoulders. As he did so, he heard the door open.

"Wha…?" Max asked, waking up.

"Someone's here," Vincent said, turning faster than his body wanted him to. If it was a demon…

It was a pixie. For a brief moment Vincent thought it was Nod. It wasn't, but Vincent still recognized her.

"Clara," he said as she flew into the room and landed on his bed.

"Who?" Max asked as he sat up.

"One of the pixies," Vincent told his brother as he walked over to her.

"Vincent, what's happened?" she asked, landing on his bed. "Where is Nod?"

Vincent returned to his bed and sat down beside her. He wasn't ready to tell her this, and he doubted he ever would be. He had to, though. She deserved to know.

"He's dead," Vincent said.

"What?" said Clara. "When? How? W…why?"

"He died saving my life," Vincent said, and he told her about the previous day. Clara listened silently, and remained silent for a few moments after he'd finished.

"I knew he was brave," Clara said, wiping the tiny tears from her face, "I just didn't realize how brave."

"Yes, he was."

Vincent and Clara turned and saw Grimbowl standing in the doorway. Vincent worried the two would start fighting, but they made no move toward each other.

"I was going to tell you this earlier, Vincent," Grimbowl said. "I think you deserve to hear it too, pixie. I ran from that house at the first sign of the demons, and met up with my tribe—remember how I told you I'd called for them, Vincent? Well, when I met them in the field, I told them what was up and suggested we run for it. Then I turned and saw your friend speeding toward us, with those three demons close behind. I knew what would happen. As soon as he saw us he'd lead the demons right to us, then escape while the demons destroyed my tribe.

"Only, he didn't. He changed direction when he saw us and led the demons away. He could have gotten away. The demons would've forgotten all about him if they'd seen us. Instead he saved my tribe. A pixie gave his life so that elves would survive. I…I never thought I'd see the day."

Vincent looked from pixie to elf, and realized he might've been witnessing the start of a beautiful friendship. Perhaps the two races could finally get along with each other, and be united by their common goal.

"You jerk!" Clara said, leaping off the bed and lunging herself at Grimbowl. The elf was surprised, but not so surprised that he didn't duck out of the way. Clara flew out the open door, and Grimbowl kicked it shut behind him.

"Damn pixies!" he said. "I'm spilling my guts here, and she..."

The door flew back open and smacked Grimbowl in the face. He flew onto Vincent's bed, right into his lap, and Clara was right behind him.

"Clara, wa..." Vincent cried before the pixie slammed Grimbowl into his chest with enough force to knock them both to the floor.

"Oww..." Vincent moaned, clutching his poor hurt chest.

"Beast!" Clara shouted, ignoring Vincent as she pounded on Grimbowl's face. His head struck Vincent's chest again and again with every blow, and Vincent howled in pain.

"Stop it!" Max yelled, springing off his bed and yanking Grimbowl off his brother just as Clara went into a body slam.

"Ooooph!" Vincent gasped as she rammed his ribs.

"Leggo!" Grimbowl said, kicking Max in the stomach.

He doubled over and fell backward, and landed bum-first on top of Clara, right into Vincent's ribs.

"Aaagh!" Vincent cried, wishing for a swift death, or at least unconsciousness.

"Get off me!" Clara shouted. She launched upward, carrying Max into the air.

And then she dropped him. Right onto Vincent's chest.

"Goooppp!" Vincent gasped, and then blissful oblivion claimed him.

• • •

He awoke an hour later to find Doctor Ritchet examining him. Vincent hurt like anything, but his pain eased when he saw Clara and Grimbowl standing on his bedside table. Both looked sheepish, and their eyes seemed to say, sorry.

"You'll be fine," the doctor told Vincent. "Just stay off your feet for the next few days, and no more rough and tumble with your brother until you are well, understand?"

Vincent nodded and turned to his brother, who sat on the edge of his own bed. Max offered him a half-smile, which did wonders for Vincent's well-being. He couldn't remember if he'd ever seen his brother smile before today.

Doctor Ritchet left the room, and Vincent turned and smiled at his friends.

"I'm okay," he told them. "But if you two start fighting again, I'll…"

He stopped, and listened. Doom, doom, doom, came a noise from the corridor, soft at first but growing steadily louder. Vincent knew he'd heard that noise before, but before he could place it, Rennik entered the room.

"That's him!" the demon said. "He's the one who infiltrated the building."

Vincent heard another couple loud and metallic dooms, and then Mr. Edwards appeared in the doorway, flanked by two bodyguards.

"Oh boy," Vincent said.

This wasn't good. Not at all.

"He's just a boy," Mr. Edwards said, his robot legs walking him into the room. "That's nay what I expected. How interesting."

Vincent pulled his bedsheets up farther, for all the good that would do him. Edwards himself looked harmless enough, and Vincent knew the demon Rennik couldn't hurt him. The two black-clad bodyguards, on the other hand, looked like they'd enjoy cracking him open. Both were big, though not as big as Barnaby Wilkins's minders, and they wore robotic-looking masks and gauntlets. They didn't appear to have guns, but Vincent suspected they had other weapons.

"Stay away from my brother!" Max said, leaping off his bed and blocking Mr. Edwards's path. "I don't know who you are, but…"

One of the bodyguards' hands snapped up, and electric bolts leapt from his gauntlet. They struck Max in the chest and threw him across the room.

"Max!" Vincent called.

"You like that?" the metal-legged man said. "We developed those gauntlets for the military, but the rest of these boys," he patted one on the back, "were built for me alone."

Oh, thought Vincent, looking closer at them. They weren't wearing robotic-looking masks at all; those were their actual faces.

"Who are you?" Vincent asked.

"My name," the metal-legged man said, "is Pharley Seamore Edwards, Chief Executive Officer of Alphega Corporation and patron of this hospital. You broke into my office tower…twice, if I understand correctly. I would like to know why."

"Actually, it was only once," Vincent replied, his eyes shifting from Edwards to Max's still form. "That first time I never got farther than the parking lot."

"That is still private property," Mr. Edwards said.

"Yeah!" added Rennik.

"Stay…away…from my brother," Max said, managing to raise his head. "And remove…the demon…from my sight."

Mr. Edwards raised an eyebrow in surprise. "You can see him? How very interesting. Most of you can nay see demons."

Something Mr. Edwards had just said nagged at Vincent's mind. Before he could think about it any further, however, the door opened and Doctor Ritchet rushed in.

"What is going on here?" the doctor asked, a split-second before one of the bodyguards grabbed him and suspended him in the air. "Wha…put me down! Put me down! Security!"

"There's no need for that," Mr. Edwards said, motioning for his minder to put the doctor down. "We are having a private discussion, and would appreciate no interruption. Is that clear?"

"But…the boy," Doctor Ritchet said, pointing at Max.

"Is that clear?" Mr. Edwards repeated.

The doctor nodded, then turned and left the room quickly.

"Is everyone afraid of you?" Vincent asked.

"They should be," Mr. Edwards said. "Just as you should not attempt to infiltrate my building ever again. I'd hate to think I might have to press charges against you…" he paused, and looked at the chart on the end of Vincent's bed, "Vincent Drear."

Vincent pushed back the covers and sat up. It hurt to do it, but Vincent wanted to address his enemy with as much dignity as he could manage. The bodyguards pointed their hands at him, but Mr. Edwards waved them down. Clearly, he saw Vincent as no immediate threat.

"Mr. Edwards," Vincent said, "if anyone here is guilty of a crime, it's you. Your demons have attacked and hurt my friends, my brother, and myself." He paused, remembering Nod. "But worse, you and your corporation are putting the whole world in danger by hiding the Portal Sites. You should be…"

"Portal Sites?" Mr. Edwards said. "My, my, don't we know a lot. Nay doubt your pixie friend told you about them before he was devoured."

Vincent's face darkened, and his hands became fists.

"That's what happens to all who oppose me," Mr. Edwards said, clearly enjoying Vincent's anger. "If you want to avoid a similar fate, I suggest you stay away. At least," his smile widened, "for the next twenty-six hours."

"You monster!" Vincent shouted, advancing a step closer. The bodyguards raised their gauntlets again, and he took that step back.

"To make sure you do keep your distance," Mr. Edwards went on, "I shall leave Rennik with you. He will keep you in line."

"He can't hurt me," Vincent pointed out.

"Not yet," Mr. Edwards replied, "but he can hurt your friends. Approach my building, and he will."

"Better believe it," Rennik said.

"He won't touch them," Vincent said. "I'll kill him first."

Mr. Edwards and Rennik laughed at that.

"Vincent Drear," Mr. Edwards said, "you can't kill Rennik, he's a demon. It is simply not possible. Demons are the most powerful, most perfect killing machines in existence. They can withstand the pressures at the bottom of the ocean, they can swim through molten lava, and they can even take the frigid emptiness of outer space. Human weapons cannot kill them; at best, they can only slow them down. There is nothing in the natural world that they cannot withstand or destroy. They are, in a word, invincible."

"So take your best shot," Rennik said, smiling wide from all the flattery.

Oh I will, Vincent thought. I will.

"So what's your evil plan, anyway?" Vincent wanted to know. "Wait until the last minute and then charge people a million bucks to use the portals?"

"No, boy," Mr. Edwards said. "My evil plan is to make sure nobody goes through. For centuries, you humans have been destroying this beautiful planet. You pollute, destroy, and create nothing but waste. And now you would walk through a Portal and leave your filth behind? I think not. You do not deserve this world. You never did. And you certainly don't deserve your one chance to escape."

Again, something nagged at Vincent. The way Mr. Edwards had said, "you humans."

"Now if you will excuse me," Mr. Edwards said, "I

have a company to run. Enjoy your day," he added as his robot legs turned him toward the door. "It is, after all, the last one you will ever have."

Vincent glared after Mr. Edwards. He desperately needed to do something, so he stumbled forward and said the first thing that came to his mind.

"Why do you eat hay?" Vincent asked.

Mr. Edwards stopped, his left foot hovering an inch above the floor. He turned around, and Vincent saw anger on his face. Anger, and even fear. Rennik, who had been leering at Vincent, turned and gave his boss a questioning glance.

"Each to their own," Mr. Edwards said, then he turned and left the room.

When Edwards and his bodyguards were gone, Vincent hobbled over to check on his brother. As he did so, Doctor Ritchet came back in.

"Are you boys all right?" he asked, crouching down beside Max.

"I'll live," Max replied.

"Not for much longer," Rennik sniggered.

"Why didn't you call security?" Vincent asked as Doctor Ritchet helped him back to his bed. "I mean, he attacked us. He should be put away."

"Mr. Edwards is a fine upstanding pillar of this community," the doctor said, turning to help Max. "And his company supplies all our equipment, medicine, and even the meals. Accusing him of a crime would mean a serious blow to this hospital. Therefore, he most certainly did not attack you."

In the corner, Rennik laughed.

"That is not the truth!" Max said as Doctor Ritchet helped him back to his bed.

"Now, now, get some rest," the doctor said. "I'll check on you boys a little later."

"Disgusting," Max said, glaring at their doctor as he hurried from the room. "That man does not Live the Life. In his soul, he is no better than that Edwards man."

"True," said Vincent. "But at least he doesn't eat hay."

"Edwards really did that?" Max asked.

"That's what I saw," Vincent replied, studying Rennik's face. The demon clearly didn't know what to make of this bit of news. For that matter, neither did Vincent.

"Why would he do that?" Max asked.

"How should I know?" Vincent replied.

Just then the door opened, and Clara flew in.

"Good news!" the pixie said. "Chanteuse is awake, and..."

She stopped, suddenly noticing Rennik. The demon looked back at her, and smiled a toothy smile.

"Dinnertime," Rennik said, and charged.

With a stomachload of dread, Vincent watched as Rennik attacked Clara. The pixie hovered in the doorway, frozen with fear. She would have died then and there, had not a Text of the Triumvirate struck Rennik in his wings.

"Got him!" Max cried triumphantly.

The blow knocked the demon down a full meter,

and he flew under the terrified pixie and through the doorway.

Clara unfroze and sped at the window, shattering it with a loud crash. Vincent got up and hurried to the door, planning to shut the demon out. He'd gotten two paces before Rennik charged back in and bolted for the broken window.

Without thinking, Vincent leapt and grabbed the demon by the right leg. It hurt to hang on, but hold on he did, and his extra weight pulled the demon away from the window and into the nearest wall. With a loud crunch Rennik bit his way through, and dragged Vincent through the hole into the next room.

The room was the same size as Vincent and Max's, and also contained two beds and a window. The beds were occupied by teenage girls, one of whom Vincent did not know. She let out a startled scream, as did Vincent when he recognized the girl in the second bed.

It was Chanteuse, and she looked terrible. Her face was bruised and bandaged, but her eyes were open and alert. Grimbowl sat beside Chanteuse, and when he saw the demon he shrieked in terror.

Rennik stopped suddenly and spun around, shaking Vincent loose. He crashed into the bedside table between the two beds, spilling the girls' breakfast tray all over himself.

"Ow!" Vincent moaned as he fell from the bedside table to the floor.

"Ow!" Rennik cried, clutching at his head. He had hurt Vincent, and his punishment was intense.

Great, Vincent thought. All I've got to do is get him to hurt me a lot, and we'll have him on the ropes in no time.

There was another loud crash as Clara burst in through the window. Rennik, who'd turned his attention to Grimbowl, looked up in time to see the pixie snatch a piece of glass from the air and jam it at him like a dagger. The impact knocked him back a meter, but the glass failed to puncture his skin. Laughing, Rennik swatted Clara away, then chased after her.

"What's going on here?" a nurse asked, poking her head through the doorway.

Clara flew at the door, then swerved left at the last second. The confused demon plowed into the door, slamming the nurse's head and knocking her cold.

"Aaagh!" Rennik cried, clutching his head while he spun around in agony. Clara grabbed the bedside table Vincent had crashed into, hauled it into the air, then used it like a battering ram to shove Rennik out of the window. Vincent heard a crunch, which he correctly guessed was the sound of the pixie stuffing the bedside table into the window, effectively blocking it up.

That won't hold Rennik long, Vincent thought as he tried to stand back up. The two girls' purses had spilled their contents on the floor, and the plastic tray had dumped its load on his bedshirt. One of the purses was definitely Chanteuse's; it was sewn by hand, and the hairspray and lipstick were made from all-natural, organic ingredients.

Those won't be useful against a demon, Vincent thought even as he scooped scrambled egg and pancakes from his chest. They're all natural...

A big thought jumped out of his head. It didn't just nag at Vincent, it grabbed him by the brain stem and shook it violently. Unfortunately, the teen girl in the other bed interrupted him.

"Where's my purse?" she said. "Hey, that's my breakfast!"

"Sorry...Lori," Vincent said, spying her nametag on the side of the other purse. "Tell you what, breakfast is on me."

He looked up and saw Clara and Grimbowl arguing with each other on Chanteuse's bed. Clara wanted to fight the demon, which would be returning momentarily to finish them off. Grimbowl was of the opinion they should run and not look back.

"Clara, Grimbowl, stop fighting and get over here," Vincent called, and grabbed a handful of scrambled egg. "Let me put this on you. It'll hide your taste before…"

The bedside table in the windowsill exploded into splinters as Rennik smashed his way through it. Clara zoomed forward and shoved Vincent back onto Lori's bed, saving him from a face full of wooden spikes.

"Hey! Get off me!" Lori said shoving Vincent off her bed. As he fell, his head whacked Clara, and in her dazed state she tumbled straight toward Rennik's open mouth.

It would have been the end of her, if Max hadn't thrown the door open and whacked Rennik on the side of the head. He spun end-over-end toward Chanteuse's bed, and landed hard on her stomach.

"Oof!" Chanteuse groaned.

"Ow!" Rennik cried, clutching his head once more.

Whump, went the sound of Clara landing on the floor, out cold.

"Vincent!" Max said, ignoring the others as he

spotted his brother. "Are you hurt?" He rushed over, stepped on something round and smooth, and fell backward onto his bum. The round and smooth thing flew forward and pinged off Vincent's face.

"Ow," Vincent whined. This just wasn't his day.

Rennik stood up on Chanteuse's stomach and spotted Grimbowl at the end of the bed. He started toward the elf, but Chanteuse sat up and grabbed his legs.

"No, you don't!" she said.

"Yes I do!" Rennik said, flapping his wings and pulling Chanteuse with him.

Grimbowl leapt off the bed onto Max, who'd just been getting up. Max fell back and Grimbowl rolled off him, then the elf made a break for the door. Miss Sloam entered just then, and Grimbowl ran straight into her. He fell back and Rennik charged, dragging Chanteuse behind him.

"Stay away from my daughter!" Miss Sloam roared, throwing a roundhouse punch into the side of Rennick's body. He flew back toward the window, his mouth closing on air, while Chanteuse lost her grip on him and fell to the floor.

"Chanteuse!" cried Miss Sloam, reaching down and

picking her daughter up. "I was so worried, I thought I would lose you."

"Oh, Mother!" Chanteuse cried and threw her arms around her mother's neck. "I'm all right."

Max helped Vincent back to his feet. Vincent was in more pain than he could stand, but hearing Chanteuse's voice again almost made him forget it. Almost. But he was as close to feeling good as it was possible for him to be.

Rennik recovered, then flew out of Miss Sloam's reach. He turned and looked down, and saw both Grimbowl and Clara lying on the floor.

"Such choice," Rennik said, his mouth open wide. "I choose...the elf!"

Vincent saw the demon start to dive, then he noticed the smooth round thing that had hit him. It had rolled across the floor to the spot where Grimbowl lay, and one word on its side grabbed Vincent's attention; aerosol.

He lunged forward, reaching for the metal can. In his mind, he saw the demon he'd squirted in the mouth with the processed cheese spray. It had acted more than just a little put out, and Vincent finally knew why. The cheese was processed, filled with chemicals.

Unnatural.

Just like this hair spray. Unlike Chanteuse's all-natural products, it was filled with environment-killing, ozone-depleting aerosol. And it even had a poison label on its side.

Rennik darted down, straight at Grimbowl's still form.

Vincent landed on top of Grimbowl, snatched up the can, and sprayed up into the demon's mouth.

"Whuth?" Rennik said, stopping just above them. At first he was merely surprised, but then he recoiled from the spray and clamped his hands over his mouth.

"Bllluuurghhh!" he cried, his mouth foaming, his wings beating so erratically he fell to the floor. Rennik's skin changed color, from fiery red to a sickly pink.

"What's going on?" Chanteuse asked as her mother set her down on the bed. "What did you do to him?"

Vincent said nothing. He tossed the can away, feeling evil for having touched it.

"Hey!" said Lori. "That's my hairspray!"

Vincent wanted to tear his eyes away from Rennik, but he could not. He felt as if he had to see this, to witness what he had done.

"What have I done?" Vincent asked the room.

"You found something that can hurt a demon,"

Clara said, sitting up on the floor where she'd landed. "And you hurt him bad."

Rennik lay on the floor, foam drooling from his mouth. His wings had shriveled up, his eyes were bloodshot and his tongue...

"Gaah," Vincent said, finally able to take no more. "No one deserves that."

"He did," Clara said. "And the elf would agree with me."

"I sure do," Grimbowl said, picking himself up off the floor. "Nice going, kid."

"What's all this?"

They turned and saw Doctor Ritchet in the doorway. He looked around the room in shock, then down at his unconscious nurse on the floor.

"Nurse!" he said, stooping down to check on her. "What happened here?"

"Oh boy," Vincent said, and tried to think of something fast.

When the nurse had been seen to, Doctor Ritchet returned to Chanteuse's room and demanded an explanation once more. In that time, Vincent's mind had been able to come up with exactly squat.

"They were throwing things all over the place," said Lori, cowering in her bed. "I saw it!"

"We were just…blowing off some steam," Max said.

"Two broken windows, a hole in the wall, damaged furniture," Doctor Ritchet said. "That looks like more than just a little…"

"Doctor Ritchet to room 308," a voice called out over the intercom. "Emergency in room 308."

"I'll expect to hear a good explanation when I get back," Doctor Ritchet said, and he hurried out the door.

And a moment later, Grimbowl darted back in.

"Sucker," he said. "That was easy!"

"That was you?" Vincent laughed.

"Mischievous creature," Chanteuse said, and there was no mistaking the smile on her face.

Vincent felt good. He was in a mountain of pain, and he might have been responsible for the death of a living creature, but seeing his hurt friend smile at the elf seemed to make everything all right. Grimbowl and Chanteuse were friends again, and all was as it should have been.

There was a commotion in the hallway, followed by several loud thumps. Vincent turned to look at the door, and his good feelings went away. Barnaby Wilkins stood there, and a moment later Bruno and Boots joined him.

Bruno held a young teen upside down in his hand: Big Tom.

Oh come on, Vincent thought. Is everyone I hate going to visit this hospital?

"There you are," said Barnaby as he entered the room. "Did we come at a bad time?" he asked, noting the destruction.

"Who're those guys?" Lori asked.

"Trouble," Vincent replied. "What do you want, Barnaby?"

"I want an explanation," Barnaby said, "for this."

Bruno hefted Big Tom higher, then waved him like a flag.

"Why did you send him to break into my house?" Barnaby asked, staring at Vincent.

"What," Vincent asked, "are you talking about?" He'd hoped he might run into Big Tom at some point, so he could apologize for beating on him yesterday. Sadly, these were not the circumstances he'd been hoping for.

"Don't play dumb," Barnaby said. "Even though you are. Big Tom said you told him to sneak into my house and steal my dad's security pass. I want to know what for."

Vincent looked up at his friend, wondering what had possessed him to break into Barnaby's house, then blame it on him. Big Tom looked back helplessly, then pointed at his nose. Vincent understood immediately; Big Tom had an obyon in his head. The elves, figuring that Vincent was out of action, had chosen a new slave. Vincent glared at Grimbowl, who shrugged.

"Don't look at me," the elf said. "I've been here all night."

"Don't feel like answering?" Barnaby said, unaware that the elf had spoken. "Okay, we do this the hard way." And he threw a fist into Vincent's stomach.

Vincent went down, the air clobbered from his lungs, preventing him from screaming. True, it was not in the chest, but it was close enough. He lay on the floor, trying to suck in air, and Barnaby smiled.

Max reacted first. He swung at Barnaby, but Boots grabbed his fist and twisted his arm behind his back. Clara took off and went for him, but Bruno lashed out his other hand and caught her like a mosquito. She struggled, but could not break free.

Even in his pain, these actions were not lost on Vincent. He can see pixies, Vincent thought. And he's stronger than her. No human being could be that strong.

"No human being is that strong," Grimbowl said, reaching the same conclusion. "Those bodyguards are trolls!"

The two bodyguards turned their heads ever so slightly and looked down at him. Grimbowl gulped, then collapsed onto the floor.

"Feel like talking now, loser?" Barnaby said, staring down at Vincent.

"Stop this at once!" Miss Sloam said as she strode forward. "You can't come in here and hurt people, this is a hospital! You let them go right now, or..."

"Shut her up," Barnaby said.

Boots nodded, and fired his right leg into Miss Sloam's chest. She crashed backward into the wall hard enough to leave an impression in the plaster, then crumpled to the floor.

"Mom!" Chanteuse cried, hurrying to help her.

"Whu...whu..." mumbled Lori, too terrified to scream.

"Woah," Barnaby said, clearly surprised at what Boots had done. "Is she...?"

"Yep," Boots replied. He looked as if he'd just signed a check or watered a plant; the fact that he'd struck a lethal blow meant nothing at all to him.

"I didn't mean…I just…wanted her quiet," Barnaby said, starting to tremble.

"And she's quiet," Boots replied.

"You monster!" Chanteuse cried.

"You wanna be next?" said Boots.

"Uh…let's just go, okay guys?" Barnaby said, backing toward the door.

"We don't have what we came for," said Bruno.

"I don't care any more," Barnaby said. "Let's just get out of here, okay?"

"No," said Bruno.

"No?" Barnaby said, forgetting his horror and shifting gears into flabbergasted. Vincent guessed, correctly, that the guards had never said no to him before.

"This kid tried to break into Alphega Corporate Headquarters," said Boots, pointing at Vincent. "Twice."

"Then he sends this twerp," said Bruno, shaking Big Tom. "He's gonna tell us why."

"I said we're leaving!" Barnaby said. "You do as I say! You're my bodyguards, and I pay you to do what I say."

"No," said Bruno. "Your father's company pays us to protect the company and its interests."

"And right now," said Boots, "finding out what this

kid knows is a higher priority than babysitting a spoiled brat."

"Don't get us wrong," said Bruno above Barnaby's sputters of outrage, "we've had some good times with you. Beating up these twerps is a lot of fun."

"But we have a duty to protect the company from any threat," said Boots. "And this kid has proven himself to be a threat. So why don't you shut your piehole and let us do our jobs?"

Barnaby's mouth opened and shut a few times as he tried to figure out what to say. In the end he said nothing and stepped back, looking utterly defeated.

"Now then," said Boots, returning his attention to Vincent. "Kid, unless you tell me how much you know, I'm going to snap off your brother's arms."

"Better yet," said Bruno, tossing Big Tom across the room and then clamping Clara in both hands, "start talking, or I squish the pixie."

Vincent sat back up. "What do you want to know?" he wheezed.

Boots opened his mouth to answer, when suddenly something hit him hard in the back of the head. He stumbled forward, surprised and clearly hurt, and reached a hand to feel his skull.

"What the…" he said, looking at his fingers. There was blood on them, his blood, from a long gash up his scalp.

Then, something hit him in the stomach. Bruno doubled over, barely keeping his grip on Clara. And then something slashed his lower arm, just below the wrist. Bruno cried out in surprise, pain, and even fear, and the hand holding Clara flew open.

Boots watched with more than a little interest as his colleague collapsed to the floor, struck down by the invisible force and Clara's unchained wrath. He stood ready, gripping Max even tighter, and prepared for a sudden attack.

"You."

He turned and saw Miss Sloam back on her feet beside him. His eyes widened in surprise, but the rest of him didn't react fast enough. Her fist plowed into his face, crumpling his dark sunglasses and breaking his nose. Boots staggered back, releasing Max as he went, then collapsed onto Lori's bed.

"Gaah," said Lori, pulling her feet out from under the thug. "This is way too freaky."

"Mom!" Chanteuse cried in surprise.

"I thought he'd killed you," Vincent added, equally surprised at her sudden recovery.

"It takes more than that," Miss Sloam said, "to kill a troll."

Chanteuse, Max, and Vincent stared at her, their astonishment reaching the level of open-mouthed shock.

"Mom?" Chanteuse said.

"It's a long story, dear," her mother said. "I was going to tell you one day, but..."

"I guess this is the day for surprises, huh?"

Everyone turned and looked. It seemed as if the voice had come from the air over Chanteuse's bed. Vincent stared, and a tiny person came into view.

"Nod!" cried Vincent.

"Nod!" cried Clara, overjoyed.

"That's right," said Nod as he peeled off the pocket he'd torn off Chanteuse's apron. "Reports of my death were just plain wrong."

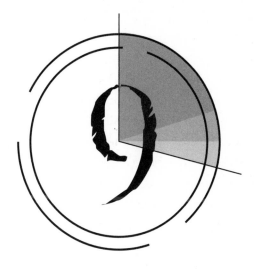

Vincent couldn't remember the last time he'd been so happy. He stared at Nod, hovering above Chanteuse's hospital bed, with a wide smile spreading over his face. He would have hugged the pixie if Nod hadn't been so small.

Clara didn't hesitate. She flung herself into Nod's arms and held him tight.

"I thought I'd lost you," she said.

"For a while there," Nod replied, "I thought I'd lost me, too."

"Impossible," Max said. "I saw the demons gaining on you."

"They nearly got me," Nod told them. "I had to use every trick in the book to stay ahead. Then I doubled back to Chanteuse's house and picked up that apron. The second I had it on, they lost me. I tore the pocket out to make it easier to wear, then I went to find you guys. Good thing I got here when I did.

"Now if you'll excuse me."

Nod peeled himself out of Clara's embrace, dropped down to the bed, and grabbed the apron pocket.

"You're leaving?" Chanteuse asked.

"Gotta keep moving," Nod said. "Once I took this thing off, I became visible on the demons' tongues again. They'll be after me again, so I've gotta scram."

"Let them come," Vincent said. "We can stop them now. Look."

Nod followed where Vincent was pointing, and saw Rennik lying in the corner. He had a moment of panic, then he realized the demon was too sick to move.

"How?" he asked, staring in amazement up at Vincent.

"I just figured it out myself," Vincent said, sitting down on the bed. His elation at the sight of his pixie friend had dissipated, and his pain was once more unbearable. "I'll tell you all about it after someone gets me some medical attention."

"Me, too," said Big Tom as he stood back up. "My head hurts."

Vincent looked over at his best friend, and smiled. Big Tom had been thrown clear across the room by a troll, but he was still standing. At least, he was standing until he tripped over Grimbowl's body and joined the elf on the floor.

"Okay, somebody tell me what's going on," Barnaby said. He stood with his back to the nearest wall, looking around the room in a state of near panic. "Who do you people keep talking to? What's all this junk about trolls?"

"You don't have the right to ask anything," Max said dangerously.

"Hey, my home was broken into!" Barnaby said. "And my bodyguards just turned traitor. I think I deserve a little slack."

"At least tell me something," said Lori from her bed. "I think I've been through quite enough today."

"Later," said Miss Sloam. "First we need a doctor in here to look after the boys, and we need security to…"

"No," said Boots. He leapt off Lori's bed, grabbed her out of it, and put her in a hammerlock in one smooth motion. Bruno sprang up and grabbed Vincent, and put him in a similar hold.

"We'll break their necks," said Bruno. "Nobody move or try to stop us."

Bruno backed toward the door, tripped on Big Tom, and fell over. Vincent flew out of his arms and crashed into Max, then moaned as his chest spiked with pain. Bruno stumbled backward and fell into the corner of the room—the same corner where Rennik the demon lay.

There was a loud, wet crunch. Against his better judgment Vincent looked, and saw a huge hole in the bodyguard's chest. Standing in that hole, looking very satisfied, was Rennik.

"Boy, I sure needed that," he said. His wings were still withered and his complexion still looked ill, but Rennik looked a lot stronger than he had a minute ago.

Boots gaped, then turned and ran. He made it into

the hallway, and then several tiny sticks rammed into his body.

"Have no fear!" Grimbowl said, leaping back up. "The cavalry's here."

Boots dropped Lori and collapsed back into the room, then fell to the floor. Lori ran off down the hall as fast as she could, screaming for security.

"Now what?" said Barnaby, who looked ready to cry.

A dozen elves came in through the doorway, all carrying tiny bows. Megon and Optar led them, climbing over the unconscious troll with a smug expression of victory.

"I thought you'd fainted," Vincent said to Grimbowl.

"Nope! Just another astral projection," Grimbowl replied. "I called in the whole tribe. And they've brought goodies."

The goodies turned out to be a magical healing potion. Optar administered it to everyone who needed it, including the two pixies. Vincent couldn't believe how quickly it worked; within seconds his chest was strong again, ribs and all.

The only ones who didn't get any were Bruno and Boots, for whom it was too late. And, of course, Rennik.

"Just a little bit?" Rennik pleaded, before he popped

Bruno's left leg into his mouth. "Please?" he added with his mouth full.

"You must be joking," Max said. "You are a creature of evil, and you will be destroyed."

"Yes, but how do we destroy them?" Megon asked as he looked at the demon. "How did you accomplish this?"

"It's the kid who figured it out," Grimbowl said with genuine pride as he indicated Vincent. "Tell 'em what you did, kid."

Vincent opened his mouth to reply, then stopped.

"No," he said.

"No?" said Grimbowl.

"No?!?" said Megon.

"I don't trust you," Vincent said. "You elves hurt me, and you made me hurt my friend Big Tom. Then you put an obyon up his nose and sent him into terrible danger."

"Oh, boo hoo," said Megon. "If you are trying to appeal to my heart, don't bother. My concern is only for my elves, and I will do whatever it takes to get them safely to the Portal Site."

"Then listen up," Vincent said. "I know where the Portal Site is."

"What?" Megon said, and a collective gasp emerged from the other elves. "Grimbowl, is this true?"

"Better believe it," Grimbowl replied.

"Tell us, boy!" Megon turned back to Vincent. "Immediately!"

"Uh, uh," Vincent said. "I'm not telling you anything unless you remove the obyon from Big Tom's nose. Immediately."

"We shall do no such thing!" Megon replied. "Who are you to make demands of us? You are lucky we don't insert obyons into all of you! In fact, I think I will..." He stopped suddenly, realizing there was a sword pressed against his throat.

"Oh no you won't," Grimbowl replied.

The other elves reacted with shock, none more so than Megon.

"In our entire history," the elf chief said, "no elf has ever raised arms against another."

"Times change," Grimbowl said. "This kid has put it on the line for us. When I first met him, I thought he was just another prat."

"Hey!" said Vincent.

"But he's done more than all of us have in a thousand years," Grimbowl went on. "If we escape this world, it'll be because of him. So stop being dumb, show him some respect, and do like he says."

There was a tense, almost silent moment. The only noise came from the corner, where Rennick was still eating troll.

"What you say," Megon said at last, "is true. He does deserve our respect. Opton, remove the obyon."

Grimbowl smiled and lowered his sword. Optar scowled, clearly not happy, but he did say the magic words to deactivate the obyon spell. Big Tom sneezed a few times, and an earwig flew out of his nose.

"You used an earwig?" Vincent said. "That's even worse. Ugh!"

"We have done our part, Vincent," Megon said. "Now it is your turn. Tell us where the Portal Site is."

"It's at Alphega Corp.'s Headquarters, hidden by the building," Vincent said. "When I did my astral projection thing, I saw all these weird force-fields surrounding the place."

"Magical wards, most likely," Optar said.

"It's also being patrolled by demons," Vincent told them.

"Then you must tell us how to destroy demons," Megon said.

"I used this on him," Vincent replied, holding the

hairspray in one hand and pointing at Rennik with the other. "It made him pretty sick."

"Aerosol sprays..." Optar said. "Of course! Human-made pollutants."

"But we need something stronger," Megon said. "Something that will kill them."

"How about bug spray?" Big Tom suggested. "We've got boxes of it back at my place."

"Of course!" Vincent said. "Big Tom, that's brilliant."

"Well, let's get going!" Grimbowl said. "We can test the spray on munchy boy, here."

Rennik, who had one of Bruno's arms sticking out of his mouth, stopped and looked at his assembled enemies. He sucked the arm in like spaghetti, smiled weakly, and ran for the window.

He didn't get far. Max caught him, and held him up by his wings.

"Lead the way, Thomas," he said.

They filed out of the room, Big Tom taking the lead. He looked happier than Vincent had ever seen him; all this positive attention was doing him good.

"Hey, Big Tom?" Vincent said, catching up to him. "Look, about what happened at school...you know, when I..."

"It's okay, Vincent," Big Tom said. "You had a thing up your nose."

"I'm still sorry," Vincent said.

"I know," Big Tom said, and smiled. "That's why I let you win."

"What?" Vincent said. "You did not. I was totally kicking your butt."

"Because I let you," Big Tom said. "I could've whupped you anytime. But I didn't, because I'm such a good friend."

Vincent laughed and put an arm around his friend's shoulders. "I guess I'm pretty lucky," he said.

"Darn right," Big Tom replied.

Chanteuse and her mother followed behind them. Miss Sloam looked very happy, no doubt glad her daughter was alive and well. Chanteuse, on the other hand, looked positively miserable.

Vincent thought he might know why, but before he could ask her the building shook violently.

"Oh no," Clara said. "It's started."

"What has started?" Max asked.

"The end!" Grimbowl replied.

And then the earthquake hit full force.

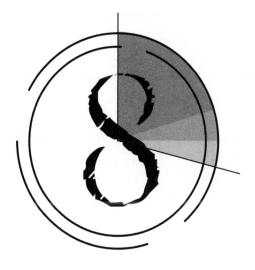

All across the world, from Antarctica to Arkansas, from Oslow to Ottawa, from Australia to Alabama, from Toledo to Tokyo, from Canada to Granada, from Moscow to Mosambique, everyone felt it. It wasn't just the Big One. It was the BIG ONE. Every land mass with a major fault line became a yawning chasm. Everywhere with a not-so-major fault line was merely reduced to a heap of rubble.

There was no doubt in anyone's mind. This was it. The end was here. Panic spread far and wide. Looting, riots, and vandalism ran rampant. War-torn nations launched sneak attacks. Doomsayers dusted off their "The End Is Nigh" sandwichboards and ran out into what remained of their streets.

Violence, chaos, mass hysteria.

And that wasn't the worst of it. The end had only just begun.

• • •

The hospital was a bombed-out wreck. Vincent and the others lay under the rubble, and Nod, Clara, and Miss Sloam were the only things keeping the rest of the building from crushing them all.

"Why," Vincent asked, shoving aside a pile of rubble, "didn't you say there'd be an earthquake?"

"I did," Nod said through his strain. "Right when we first met, remember?" He still wore the apron pocket; if Vincent didn't focus on him, his burden of debris appeared to be held up by nothing.

"I could have used a reminder," Vincent told him.

When the building fell apart, they'd dropped down

through the crumbling floor while the ceiling and floors above chased them. They'd sustained many injuries when they'd landed; Vincent had broken both legs, Max had been impaled on a steel support rod and Barnaby had fractured his skull. Only Big Tom and Chanteuse missed the worst of it; the elves had put them to work immediately distributing their healing potion.

Sadly, the potion hadn't come in time for several elves, including Megon. Falling debris had crushed them; only the quick actions of Miss Sloam and the two pixies had prevented any further deaths.

"What are those things?" Barnaby asked, finally able to see the pixies and elves.

"Our friends," Vincent replied. "Except him," he added as Rennik popped out of the rubble beside him. A steel girder and at least two tons of cement had fallen on the sickly demon, but he was still able to chomp.

"Won't be long now!" Rennik said. "First the earthquake, then the bad weather, and then…"

"There's bad weather coming?" Big Tom asked.

"Priorities, people!" Clara cried through clenched teeth. She hovered above Max with a chunk of building pressing down on her, and she was slowly dropping. Nod held aloft a similar load above the remaining elves, but his strength was also fading. Miss Sloam, who shouldered the biggest burden, looked as if she couldn't go on for one more moment.

Vincent looked around. There were piles of rubble everywhere, blocking every escape route. They were trapped. And as soon as their friends' strength gave out, they were dead.

"We're dead!" Barnaby said. "We're all dead! There's no way out, we're going to die..."

"Shut up," Vincent said, and slugged him. Barnaby was so surprised he sat looking at Vincent for almost five seconds before he fell backward onto Grimbowl and Optar.

Vincent allowed himself a moment. That felt good.

"Watch where you hit people!" Grimbowl said from under the stunned bully. Vincent watched as he crawled out, and then he had a thought.

Vincent looked at the hole Rennik had eaten his way up from. Then he looked at Rennik.

"You can get us out of here," he told the demon. "You can eat your way through this rubble."

"Hey, yeah, I could," Rennik said. "But why should I? You tried to kill me, remember?"

"You tried to eat my friend," Vincent reminded him. "Besides, don't you want to eat us later?"

"Well…"

"Hard to do that if we're under a ton of rubble," Vincent said. "If you free us, you'll have a chance to eat us when the epoch ends."

"True," Rennik said, "But I can't chase you with these wings. And your poison made me too weak to move. I couldn't save you if I wanted to.

"Unless," he added, "you gave me some of that healing potion."

"What?" said Vincent.

"Not going to happen," said Grimbowl.

"Never!" added Optar.

"Then I guess we're all stuck here," Rennik said.

"Optar," Vincent said, "we are going to die. He can save us. Give him what he wants."

Optar looked at Vincent, then at Grimbowl. They nodded to each other, then Optar took a flask off his belt.

"Give him this," Optar said, handing Vincent the tiny flask.

Vincent handed the potion to Rennik, who took it and poured the contents into his mouth.

"Ahhh, that's the stuff," he said as he healed before

them. His wings became strong and powerful, and his skin turned red once more. "I'm back!"

"Now get us out of here," Max told him.

"Forget it," Rennik said, hopping into the air. "Now that you've cured me, I'm going to eat you all, starting with her!" He pointed at Miss Sloam.

"No!" Chanteuse said, leaping to protect her mother.

"No!" Vincent cried, realizing he'd been duped.

"Yes!" Rennik said, and he sped toward his target.

"Demon, stop!" Optar shouted.

Rennik ignored him, and he'd almost made it to Miss Sloam's left arm when he screamed and fell to the ground.

"You will not attack us," Optar commanded. "And you will clear this debris. Immediately!"

Rennik screamed again, clutching at his body. Then he got up and obeyed the elf.

"Obyon?" Vincent asked the wise elf.

"Got it in one," Grimbowl said.

"You didn't think I'd heal that dog," Optar said, "without first giving him a leash?"

It took Rennik two minutes to clear away all the rubble, including the detritus piled on top of Nod,

Clara, and Miss Sloam. Freed from their burdens, the troll and both pixies collapsed with exhaustion. While Chanteuse helped her mother to the floor, Vincent collected up Clara and Nod. Finding Nod wasn't easy; Vincent had to pat around with his hands before he found the nigh-invisible pixie.

Rennik coughed and spat, clearing out the concrete from his mouth. The taste clearly wasn't to his liking.

"We're free!" Big Tom said, smiling widely. Then he looked around and his smile dropped.

"Oh man," Vincent said.

"Triumvirate, be merciful," Max added.

The city was devastated. Buildings lay in ruins beneath clouds of dust, cars and trucks lay smashed and mangled, and the streets were cracked and broken beyond all hope of repair. Fires blazed, broken hydrants fountained, and car alarms howled. It was a nightmare brought to life, and death was all it gave in return.

"The Text said there would come times like these," Max said.

"I know," Vincent said. "Something about wailing and gnashing teeth, right?"

In fact, more than half of the Text of the Triumvirate dealt with the End Times. It was the most popular subject for sermons, the most successful tool for recruiting new members, and the only topic dealt with in the many books and videos produced by the Triumvirite media.

Vincent remembered well being forced to sit through a screening of Left Out, a cheesy and overly melodramatic drama about the people who were not taken to Heaven by the Triumvirate during the Latter Days. Those poor souls faced famine and wars while the evil Anti-Triumvirate took over the world. Those non-Triumvirites had to fight for their very survival, while Vincent had fought to stay awake.

Now, he doubted he'd have the chance to sleep again. Left Out, and its many poor-production-value imitators, had not prepared him for this.

"We should have missed this," Grimbowl said. "All of us, everyone, should have avoided this."

"All because of one evil man," Max added. "And those who serve him."

"Yeah, it's pretty lousy," Rennik said. "Now, if you'll excuse me..."

"Demon, bring the troll," Optar said. "You will accompany us to Big Tom's house, where you will tell us everything."

"Oh, no," the demon muttered as he grabbed hold of Miss Sloam and lifted her into the air. "Can this day get any worse?"

"You bet it can," Grimbowl replied. "After you've told us all you know, you're going to be our guinea pig."

"What are you saying?" asked Chanteuse.

"He's going to help us find out," Grimbowl said, "if Big Tom's bug spray can kill demons."

Big Tom's house was surprisingly undemolished. It was damaged, of course, and the inside was a mess of fallen dishes and overturned furniture. The house itself remained standing, however, like most of the homes in Big Tom's neighborhood. Being so small and dilapidated anyway, there wasn't much left for the earthquake to do.

His parents weren't at home. Both had two jobs, and would have been at one or the other when the quake hit. With the phone lines down, there was no way to find out if they had survived. The same was true, Vincent realized, of his own parents. Even Barnaby looked close to tears at the possible fate of his father.

They set up camp in Big Tom's basement. Grimbowl stood guard over Rennik, who'd been ordered not to move the moment they arrived. Optar stood before the demon and asked him questions about Alphega Corp. Rennik answered the questions, but his attention was focused on the corner of the room where several boxes were stacked. Some of the boxes had fallen and broken open, and cans of bug spray lay scattered around on the floor. Rennik eyed them with obvious terror; every single can appeared to be intact and usable.

Chanteuse's mother looked after the pixies, laying them down on a small, grubby mattress that turned out to be Big Tom's bed. Vincent, Big Tom, and Barnaby sat on the other end of the mattress, watching the interrogation. Rennik spoke a lot of strange mumbo jumbo that made no sense to the boys but seemed perfectly clear to the elves.

Vincent looked around, and noticed Chanteuse

and Max weren't downstairs with the rest of them. He heard a noise from the main floor, so he went upstairs to investigate.

Halfway up he found Max sat on the stairs, reading a book. Vincent blinked in surprise; it was the very same book Max had once scolded Vincent and Big Tom for reading. It was the *Prisons & Poltergeists Book of Creatures*, a volume of information that supplemented the Prisons & Poltergeists role-playing game.

Vincent and Big Tom had never actually played—the Triumvirate forbade it, and Big Tom couldn't afford all the extra materials. Big Tom had acquired the book as a birthday present from a cousin who had given up the game and wanted to get rid of his books. Big Tom had brought it over one day to show Vincent, and when Max had seen them reading it he'd raised an almighty stink.

"'Beware yea of doctrines of demons,'" Max had quoted, "'lest they lead your soul astray.'"

And now he was reading it. Filling his mind with evil images, as it were. Vincent could have pointed this out, but the look on his brother's face changed his mind.

"What's wrong, Max?" he asked, sitting down beside him.

"Oh, hello Vincent," Max said. "I was just…trying to understand."

"Understand what?" Vincent asked, but he suspected he already knew the answer. Max's worldview had taken a tremendous pounding over the last day and a half, after all.

"These creatures," Max said. "This book talks about pixies and trolls and elves. Look here," he tapped a picture of a creature with the body of a horse, but the upper half of a man where its head should have been. "This is a centaur."

"Nod and Clara told me about centaurs," Vincent said, looking at the picture. "So that's what they look like."

"It says here they are very intelligent and spiritual creatures," Max went on, "but also headstrong, arrogant, and set in their ways. I'm like this centaur, aren't I?"

Vincent opened his mouth to speak, then chose to say nothing once more.

"I was arrogant," Max told him. "I thought I knew everything. What was good, what was evil," he tapped the book and gave a small smile, acknowledging their past dispute. "Lately, however, the Triumvirate have opened my eyes. And they did it through you, Vincent."

"Me?" Vincent asked.

"You brought me into this," Max reminded him. "Thanks to you, I learned there is so much more to life than I'd thought. Creatures I'd believed evil, people like your friend Chanteuse. She's a witch, but she is such a good soul. I just..." He waved the book while searching for words. "I just want to understand this new world."

"It's not that new," Vincent pointed out. "Okay, the world is about to end, that's new. Except it isn't, it's been going on for epochs now...The point is, creatures like Nod and Grimbowl have been here for a long time. And if the Triumvirate are really all-powerful..."

"Of course they are!" Max snapped.

"...then they know all about pixies and elves and centaurs, too," Vincent finished. "So it's all okay."

Max stared at his brother for a long moment, then shook his head.

"I never thought I would say this," he said, "but you are very wise, little brother."

Vincent blushed, and felt a tear forming in his left eye. That was the nicest thing his brother had ever said to him.

"Keep reading," Vincent said. "I'm going to go check on Chanteuse."

• • •

Chanteuse was making tea. She'd waded across a floor so dirty the broken dishes and spilled cutlery were hardly noticeable. She held the kettle in the sink, and was trying to get water out of the taps when Vincent found her. On the kitchen counter was a box of the cheapest tea available. It was high in caffeine and low on taste, and was the type of tea Chanteuse would never drink even if the world were ending. Which of course it was.

"What's wrong?" Vincent asked. He'd expected she would be catching up with her mother. It wasn't every day you learned your mom was a troll, after all.

"There doesn't seem to be any water," Chanteuse said, twisting the taps off. "Perhaps they have some bottled water in the fridge."

"Not likely," Vincent said. "Not when it's free out of the tap. Big Tom's family never had money for that kind of stuff. They even eat their cereal with tapwater."

"They seem to have plenty of money for insect spray," she said, her voice harsh.

Vincent thought he understood what was troubling her. When he'd sneezed out his obyon, she had set the ladybug free. Chanteuse loved the natural world, and considered the killing of bugs to be wrong.

"They really do hate cockroaches," Vincent said,

watching as one scuttled across the floor. "But we won't use it on bugs. We're going to..."

"You're going to kill that helpless creature downstairs," Chanteuse said, still with her back to him.

"You mean Rennik?" Vincent said. "But he's a demon. He's bad. They all are."

"They are living creatures, Vincent!" Chanteuse said, turning and facing him. Her eyes blazed with such fury that Vincent took an involuntary step back. "Bad or not, they are part of the natural world. They serve a function, horrible though it might be, and we have no right to kill them."

Vincent gulped, but then he straightened and stood tall. He'd learned to stand up to his many enemies over the years, but standing up to a friend was much harder. Seeing her like this was heartbreaking, but that didn't change the way things were. Or what had to be done.

"Chanteuse," Vincent said, "these living-thing-part-of-the-natural-world creatures' function is to exterminate all life as we know it. Natural or not, they are bad news. And in case you didn't realize it, we are part of the natural world, too. We deserve to survive just as much as they do."

"Do we?" Chanteuse asked him. "Humans have been

polluting and destroying this planet for centuries, Vincent. We've destroyed rainforests and our ozone layer, we've driven entire species to extinction, we've taken every gift Mother Earth has given us and spoiled them, then thrown them back in Her face. Perhaps," she turned away, paused. "Perhaps we don't deserve to survive."

Vincent thought about that for a moment.

"Yes we do, Chanteuse," he said. "We have just as much right to survive as every other animal. Yes, we pollute. Yes, we fight. But we've accomplished so much. We've traveled around the solar system, we've developed great technology..."

"And what has all that gotten us?" Chanteuse said. "Haven't I taught you anything, Vincent? Human beings have abandoned their natural roots, forgotten how to commune with nature..."

"Because that's the way we are," Barnaby said as he emerged from the stairwell, causing Vincent and Chanteuse to jump. "Man, you Mother Earth-loving tree-huggers make me sick. It's called progress, lady. Survival of the fittest."

"Nobody asked you for your opinion, jerkwad," Vincent said.

"Well, you're getting it," Barnaby said, pushing past

him to face Chanteuse. "We humans have one purpose, and one purpose alone: survival. Sometimes bad things have to be done to make sure we survive, like chopping down trees for wood or nuking people before they nuke us. And don't give me that garbage about forgetting our natural roots. We don't have any. We evolved because we were the strongest species around. And if we can find a way to survive now, it's because we're still the strongest."

"You poor child," Chanteuse said. "Have you no compassion for anything?"

"Nope," Barnaby said. "You can't spend compassion. I'm out for number one. And that's why I'll survive while you get eaten by the demons you're trying to save."

Chanteuse opened her mouth to speak, then closed it. What could she say?

"At least she cares," Vincent said. "Which is more than I can say for you."

"That's my point, loser," Barnaby said. "I don't care, and if you want to get off this rock before more demons come, you'd better ditch the witch and think about your own skin."

Barnaby turned and went back downstairs, stepping on a cockroach as he did so. Vincent resisted the urge to slug him, and asked himself again why he'd let Barnaby tag along. It had just seemed wrong to abandon him after they'd escaped the ruined hospital. They all stood a better chance of survival if they stuck together, Vincent knew, so Barnaby would probably die if made to fend for himself. He'd lost his bodyguards and possibly his father, so allowing Barnaby into the group was the moral choice. If only the jerk would pretend to be grateful for it.

And, jerk though Barnaby was, Vincent couldn't ignore what he'd said.

"He's got a point," he told Chanteuse. "We have to look out for ourselves. I want to live through this, and I'm sure you do, too."

"Not if it means hurting other creatures," she replied. "That is wrong, Vincent. And I want no part of it."

Chanteuse turned back to her tea. Vincent stared helplessly at her back a few moments longer, then he turned and went back down the stairs.

"Aww," said Barnaby. "Did you and the nature freak break up?"

"Shut up," Vincent said, glaring at him.

"Or what?" Barnaby challenged, smiling his patented bully smirk.

"Or we'll kick your butt," Big Tom said, walking over to Vincent's side.

"Nah, he's not worth it," Vincent said. "Besides, I already punched him out once today, remember? That didn't improve him at all."

"Come on, Vincent," Big Tom said. "We owe him a knuckle sandwich."

"That won't solve anything," Vincent said.

"It'll make us feel better," Big Tom said.

Vincent thought about that for a moment.

"Good point," he said. "Shall we?"

"Hey, wait a second…" Barnaby said, his smirk vanishing as Vincent and Big Tom laid into him with both fists.

"Keep it down, you two," Clara called over her shoulder.

"Try to beat him up quietly," Nod added.

Barnaby tried to fight back, but without his bodyguards he was no match at all. He covered his head with his arms and whimpered, probably wishing it would end soon.

"Cut that out," said Miss Sloam, grabbing both boys by the backs of their shirts and hauling them into the air. "We've got enough problems without you boys fighting. If you must, take it outside."

The wind chose that moment to howl menacingly.

A blast of thunder came a moment later, and the house shook.

"Nah, we're done," Big Tom said, and Miss Sloam released them.

The wind howled again, and then the rain came. It hammered the house like machine gun bullets, but wasn't loud enough to cover a deafening boom of thunder.

"Uh oh," Clara said, flying to the window. "The bad weather has started."

"What was your first clue?" Grimbowl asked.

Here we go, Vincent thought. From here on out, it's going to be one long series of mad dashes to the finish line. He could only hope and pray the finish line would still be there when they arrived.

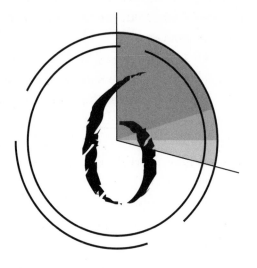

The power blinked on and off as the lightning strikes got closer and closer. The group, with the exception of Chanteuse, huddled in the basement of Big Tom's house, planning their next move.

"Time is running out," Optar said. "If we are to

make an attempt on getting through the portal, we must go now, before the weather gets any worse."

"And it will," said Nod, sitting up on the mattress. "Once the tornadoes start…"

"We get the idea," Vincent said.

"The demon has revealed to me what we must do," Optar said. "It seems the Alphega building is surrounded by several magical wards."

"What do they do?" Vincent asked, remembering the force-fields he'd seen when he'd visited the building in spirit.

"They block the calling of the portals," Optar said. "That's why nobody knows about them. Apparently Alphega Corp. has built structures around all the Portal Sites on the planet, and each one is blocked by similar wards.

"But here's the thing," Optar continued. "All the wards are connected together. If we can bring them down here, then they will fall all across the world."

"Wow," Vincent said. "If we did that, we might actually save a lot of people."

"Goodie-goodies," Barnaby muttered.

"You want some more?" Big Tom asked, raising his fists.

Barnaby kept silent.

"How do we take down the wards?" Vincent asked.

"We'll explain on the way," Optar said, opening a box full of spray cans. "Everyone load up on these and let's go."

"Not so fast," Grimbowl said. "We still need to see if the spray will actually work. And that means you," he turned to Rennik.

"Gulp," the demon replied.

Vincent sighed. He'd hoped they could just leave and forget about testing the spray on Rennik. True, the demon was a nasty piece of work. However, Chanteuse was right—he was a living thing. Vincent didn't think he could simply kill him in cold blood.

"Why don't you do it, Vincent," Grimbowl said, hopping onto a box and tossing him a can. "Only fair. You're the one who brought us all together, after all. Demon," he turned back to Rennik, "open your mouth. Wide."

Rennik resisted for a moment, then cried out in pain and opened his mouth as far as it would go.

"Go for it," Grimbowl said to Vincent, offering him a bright smile.

"Yes, go for it, Vincent," said Chanteuse as she

came down the stairs. She eyed Vincent with contempt, certain he was about to commit murder.

"It is the will of the Triumvirate that these beasts be put to death," Max said, sensing his brother's hesitation. "Make Mother and Father proud. Kill it."

Vincent looked down into the gaping maw of Rennik, who pulled his tongue as far back as he could manage. His teeth still looked deadly fearsome; if Vincent didn't know for sure the demon was helpless, he wouldn't have come so close.

He wasn't a good creature. Rennik had betrayed him, and only Optar's savvy had saved them from death in the hospital ruins. If Vincent spared the demon, he knew there would be no thanks. Worse, Rennik would do everything in his power to kill them all if he was left alive. He was a threat, a very real danger.

But his eyes told a different story. Wide with terror, they were the eyes of a creature who just wanted to live.

"Come on, Vincent," Nod said.

"Just do it," Clara added.

"Wimp," said Barnaby.

Vincent stood there looking at the can. This was his decision to make, whether or not to attempt the murder of a creature he'd already tried to kill with hairspray.

It should have been simple, and almost everyone was urging him to do it. Of course, that was peer pressure talking, and caving to that sort of thing had never been Vincent's failing.

He looked up at Chanteuse, saw the look in her eyes, and knew what he had to do.

"No," said Vincent. "No, I won't do it."

"What?" said Grimbowl. "Vincent, that demon…"

"I'm not a murderer," Vincent said.

"Oh brother," Barnaby said, walking forward. "Here, I'll do it."

"You will not," Vincent said. "None of you will. It's wrong."

"Vincent is right," Chanteuse said, striding forward and standing beside him. "I'm proud of him, and ashamed of all of you! Stop this at once."

"But Chanteuse," Grimbowl said, "we have to test the spray."

"No," Chanteuse said. "It is wrong."

"No it is not!" Optar said.

"Not if it's done in the name of the Triumvirate!" Max added. "All acts done in their Blessed and Holy names are right and just, and may the Triumvirite strike me down if it is otherwise."

Just then, a two-by-four slammed through the basement window and missed Max's head by an inch.

"What the..." Vincent said, staring as the wooden plank of death imbedded itself in the far wall.

"Tornado," Big Tom said, looking through the shattered window. "And it's coming this way."

"Everyone against the wall!" Miss Sloam shouted. They rushed to the wall and crouched down beside it, then waited for the tornado to pass. Miss Sloam held her daughter close, Max held on to Vincent and Big Tom, the pixies and the elves laid themselves flat on the floor, and Barnaby burrowed under the mattress.

The house shook. Violently. Vincent huddled closer to his brother, hoping the ordeal would be over soon. Which, in a few hours, it would be.

Over the howling wind and the shaking of the house, Vincent could just make out another series of sounds. Sort of a rip, whip, clatter. Vincent's curiosity overrode his terror and he looked up, searching for the source of the noise.

He saw Rennik on the other side of the room, next to the spray can boxes. The demon picked one up, ripped it open, and whipped it through the open window. Vincent could clearly see the wind snatching the cans out of the box, blowing them away with a clattering sound.

Rennik was already on to the next box, and there were very few boxes left. And it didn't take Vincent long at all to realize what that meant.

"Stop!" Vincent cried, leaping up and charging toward the demon. "Optar, make him stop."

"Demon!" the elf elder said. "I order you to…" He never finished, because Rennik threw a box at him, knocking him over.

"You little jerk!" Vincent said, snatching up a can and pointing it at Rennik. "I can't believe I felt bad about killing you before."

"What's stopping you now, human?" Rennik said. "Face it, you couldn't kill me then, and you are too weak to do it now. And if you can't do it," he picked up the last box, "you can't stop me."

"I can!" said Grimbowl, standing back up. "Demon, I order you…"

And then the house blew down. Literally. It tore right off its foundations and blew away, leaving the basement exposed to the rain, wind, and debris from the massive tornado tearing past less than a block away.

"Woah!" cried Nod and Clara as the winds sent them flying.

"No!" Chanteuse cried, leaping for them with her arms outstretched and only just missing.

"Yum!" said Rennik, leaping to intercept them with his mouth open wide.

"No!" cried Vincent as the two pixies fell straight into the demon's maw. Nod and Clara threw their tiny arms and legs up and fought against Rennik's jaws, but it was clearly a losing battle.

Vincent leapt into action. He'd lost Nod once, and wasn't about to do so again. He jammed the can of bug spray into the demon's mouth and fired off a long burst.

The effect was instantaneous. Rennik's skin went pale, then started to melt off. He aged visibly, lines and wrinkles forming on his skin even as it dripped off him. His wings withered to twigs and snapped off, and he fell to the floor with a wet splat. Clara and Nod threw open his mouth and flew out, then wiped at the frothy spray on their bodies.

"Great shot, kid!" Grimbowl cried. "We know the stuff works now, don't we?"

Vincent didn't reply. He watched what was left of

Rennik melt into a technicolor puddle, then turned away in disgust.

"You had to do it," Chanteuse said, taking his hand. "You saved the pixies' lives."

"I know," Vincent replied, giving her hand a squeeze. "Just don't expect me to like it."

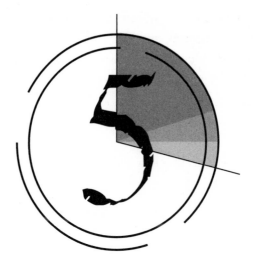

While Nod and Clara flew off to collect any salvageable spray cans, the elves, humans, and troll sat in a circle and discussed strategy.

"We still don't have any way to get there," Grimbowl said. "It could take days to walk to the Portal Site."

"Days we don't have," Vincent said. "The pixies could probably carry a few of us, but not all."

"Do any of your neighbours have SUVs?" Chanteuse asked Big Tom, and all eyes stared at her incredulously. "Well, yes, they ruin the environment and I hate them, but they could probably manage the trip through the city."

"None of my neighbors have any," Big Tom said sadly.

"Poor bum," Barnaby said. "My dad has one."

"Is it here?" Vincent asked.

"No," Barnaby replied.

"Then shut up," Vincent said. "We only want helpful suggestions."

"I fear only the gods can help us now," Optar sighed.

Vincent looked at Max.

And Max looked at Vincent.

"The Gods!" Vincent said. "The protest is today!"

"And it's only a couple of kilometers from here," Max added.

"What are you two talking about?" Grimbowl asked.

"Gods," Vincent said. "Global Outland Drivers. The new off-road utility vehicle from Regular Engines."

"They are premiering them today," Max said, "at special car shows all across the world."

"Our parents and their church were going to lead a protest out front," Vincent said. "They don't think anyone or anything should use the name 'god' except for God."

"And they're right," Max said. "But under the circumstances I think the Triumvirate would want us to use them."

"Yeah?" said Barnaby. "Are they here?"

"No," said Vincent.

"Then why don't you shut up?" Barnaby said smugly.

"They're at the South Gates shopping mall," Vincent told him.

"That's not far from here," Chanteuse said.

"Exactly," said Vincent, smugly.

"It's a longshot," Grimbowl said. "With the earthquake and now the tornadoes, there might not be any of those God things left."

"It's our best shot," Vincent said.

"And we'd be able to rescue Mother and Father," Max said, "and anyone else who turned up for the event."

"Uh, kid?" Grimbowl said. "With all that's been

going on outside, do you really think they would go ahead with their protest?"

Max looked at Vincent.

And Vincent looked at Max.

"Without a doubt," Max said.

"Yeah," Vincent agreed. "These natural disasters will only encourage them."

• • •

The walk to the South Gates Mall was treacherous, to say the least. Tornadoes continued cutting the city to ribbons; several times they had to seek shelter from raining debris.

"Keep your heads down," Miss Sloam said, swatting aside a plummeting fast-food restaurant sign with a downed streetlamp. "And stay close to the buildings. We don't want anyone getting sucked away by a twister."

"Except maybe Barnaby," Big Tom said, and Vincent snickered.

Luckily, the only tornado in the immediate area was heading away from them in a south-easterly direction. Vincent crossed his fingers and hoped their luck would hold.

As the twister moved off and the wind died down, the group heard a voice in the distance. They couldn't make anything out at first, but as they got closer to the mall the voice became recognizable.

"You have got to be kidding me," said Barnaby.

"…and to those who would claim divinity simply by merit of their ABS brakes, four-wheel drive, and 5.5% financing, I say blasphemy!" came the unmistakable voice of Vincent's father. "To those who would tempt us with air conditioning, power steering, and roomy interiors if we would but fall to our knees and call them gods…"

"Come on," said Vincent, embarrassed but determined. "Let's go crash us a protest."

One block later, they arrived at the mall parking lot. Ahead was a scene of utter devastation; it was obvious a tornado had torn right through the mall's center. Goods of all kinds lay scattered everywhere, from the latest in fashion to the cheapest of dollar-store knickknacks.

And in the middle of the mess—in some ways covered by it—was the protest. It was small, with fewer than five people in attendance. Likely there had been more when the event started, but Vincent guessed the majority had lost their faith when the world came apart.

"Do not be discouraged by the evidence of the Triumvirate's wrath," Mr. Drear spoke into his megaphone as he stood atop an overturned God. "They are testing our resolve, even as they seek to punish those who would drive these abominations."

Vincent wanted to crawl into a hole and die. Big Tom and Chanteuse looked at him with sympathy. Barnaby laughed out loud. And Max beamed with pride.

"Despite all else, Father fights to spread the Word," he said.

"Oh man," Barnaby said. "This explains so much."

"You want another pounding?" Vincent asked him. "Didn't think so. Grimbowl, Max, come with me. The rest of you, find us some working Gods."

"And what are we going to do?" Grimbowl asked.

"The hard part," Vincent said. "Convince my parents to come with us."

Vincent, Max, and Grimbowl approached the Triumvirates. Vincent thought hard about what he would say. After all, an earthquake and a few tornadoes hadn't convinced them to pack up and move on. What could he possibly come up with to get through to them?

As they approached, Mr. Drear looked down and saw them. His face brightened in astonished delight, and he leapt down from the overturned SUV and hurried toward them.

"Max!" Mr. Drear cried, embracing his firstborn in a bear hug. "Max, my boy, you're all right! We feared you'd been killed!"

"I am all right, Father," Max said, hugging him back. "I am glad you are also unharmed."

"I'm okay too," Vincent said bitterly.

"Vincent! Max!" Mrs. Drear cried, throwing down her picket sign and scooping the three of them up in an embrace. Vincent hugged back happily, relieved. Both his parents had survived.

"I hate to break up this touching moment," Grimbowl said, "but time is…"

"Demon!" Mr. Drear said, pushing his wife and sons away and swinging a kick at the elf.

"Dad, no!" Vincent cried as Grimbowl ducked under Mr. Drear's leg.

"Stop that," Grimbowl said, delivering a kick of his own.

Mr. Drear yelped and clutched his shin. Vincent winced; he knew how much that hurt.

"Grimbowl, back off," he said. "You too, Dad. He's not a demon."

"Is it another angel?" Mrs. Drear asked.

"Do not be fooled," Mr. Drear said. "It has enslaved Vincent's mind, and now it seeks to enslave ours!"

"He is not a demon," Max said.

"Oh?" said his father.

"The Triumvirate have opened my eyes to his true nature," Max said, "and revealed him to be a friend.

"It was Vincent who introduced me to them," Max went on. "At first I thought the same as you, that he must be a creature of evil. Then I met the real demons, and I joined with my brother and creatures like this one in fighting them."

Mr. Drear looked down at his other son, astonishment back on his face.

"All this time," he said, "you, Vincent, have been fighting demons?"

"Yep," Vincent replied.

"Triumvirate forgive me," his father said. "I had no idea."

Wow, Vincent thought. That's as close to an apology as I'll ever get.

"We have to go," he said, taking his father's hand.

"But the protest…" Mr. Drear said.

"There is another protest you must attend to," Max said. "Vincent has found the demons' lair. We must journey there with our friends and allies to confront these wicked creatures and destroy them."

Mr. Drear shook his head. We're losing him, Vincent thought.

"This is the most important protest in the world," Vincent said, and then he had a brainstorm. "And, none of the other religious groups know about it."

Mr. Drear's eyes widened.

"We'd be the first?" he said.

"Uh huh," Vincent nodded.

Mr. Drear looked at Max, then at his wife, then at Vincent. Then back to Max.

"You must come now, father," Max said. "Time is short."

"Very well, son," Mr. Drear said. "Lead the way."

• • •

Vincent felt good as he and Max led their parents into the nearby lot to find the others. His spirits dropped, however, when he saw the state the Gods were in. Some had been crushed by debris, while others had been blown away by the tornadoes. When they met up with the others, Vincent's worst fears were confirmed.

"They're all busted," Barnaby said. "Good plan, loser."

"I'm afraid he's right," Chanteuse said as she came around the side of an overturned God. "They are all…"

"The witch!" Mr. Drear barked. "What is she doing here?"

Oh no, Vincent thought, cursing himself for not seeing that one coming.

"She is all right, father," Max said.

"She most certainly is not!" Mr. Drear shouted. "These creatures I can accept," he waved a hand at the elves, "since you clearly control them…"

"Hey!" said Grimbowl.

"How dare you!" said Optar.

"…but this person," Mr. Drear went on, returning his contemptuous gaze to Chanteuse, "is an abomination, and…"

"What," bellowed Miss Sloam from right behind him, "did you just call my daughter?"

"Um," said Mr. Drear, staring up at her angry face.

"Let me put this up his nose," Optar said, pulling a bug from his pouch. "We'll see who controls who!"

"Stop!" shouted Big Tom, in the biggest voice Vincent had ever heard from him. "Listen, can you hear that?"

"Hear what?" Barnaby asked, and then he heard it. Then they all heard it.

"Helicopters!" said Mrs. Drear.

And indeed they were. Three choppers appeared on the horizon and came in fast. Two took up flanking positions in the air while the middle helicopter descended slowly to the parking lot.

"We're saved," Mrs. Drear said.

"Don't be so sure," said Vincent. "That's the Alphega symbol on the side of those coptors."

"It's my dad!" Barnaby said. "He's come to get me."

"What about the rest of us?" asked Miss Sloam.

"Oh, I'm sure they'll rescue you, too," Barnaby said.

Vincent wasn't so sure.

"Optar?" he whispered, getting down on one knee. "You have any obyons left?"

"Plenty," the elf replied. "You think we'll need them?"

"Maybe," Vincent said. "Nod?"

"Right here," the near-invisible pixie said, landing on Vincent's shoulder.

"Good," Vincent said. "Listen up, here's the plan…"

When Vincent stood back up, the helicopter had landed. Mr. Wilkins climbed out and walked toward them, accompanied by four troopers. On his right hand, Vincent noted with interest, he wore a gauntlet identical to the ones worn by Mr. Edwards's robotic bodyguards.

"Barnaby!" Mr. Wilkins said, taking hold of his son. "You made it. But then, I knew you would. We Wilkinses are made of stern stuff."

"We sure are, Dad," Barnaby replied. "How did you find me?"

"You have a homing device on you," Mr. Wilkins said. "I didn't trust my boss Edwards to rescue you when things went bad, so I took precautions. I would have come for you sooner, but the tornadoes made flying impossible."

"So you knew what was coming," Chanteuse said, "yet you didn't warn anyone, even your son."

"Who are these people?" Wilkins asked, gesturing with his gloved hand. "I see elves, one pixie, and…is that a troll?"

"That's her mom," Barnaby said, pointing at Chanteuse.

"She could almost pass for human," Wilkins said. "Though certainly not a pretty one."

"How dare you!" Chanteuse said, and Miss Sloam took a threatening step forward.

"Stay where you are," Wilkins said dangerously. He raised his gloved hand, and his troopers aimed their weapons.

"Do as he says," Vincent said. "Those gloves hurt."

"Smart boy," Wilkins said. "I remember you. You're the one that wanted to befriend my Barnaby. Tell me, son, did he pass the test?"

"Nope," Banraby said with a wide, evil grin. "And his friends here took me hostage."

"We did not!" Max shouted.

"We saved his life," Grimbowl added.

"Enough of this!" Mr. Drear said, pushing his way to the front of the group. "We are Triumvirites, sir, and are on a quest to spread the Sacred Truth. We need transport, and the Triumvirate have delivered you and your helicopters unto us. Will you give us passage?"

"Let me consider that," Wilkins said. "No."

"No?" Mr. Drear asked. "But you were sent to us in our hour of need!"

"I came here to collect my son," Wilkins said. "That is all. I can think of no reason why I should transport any of you anywhere. Can you, Barnaby?"

"Nope," Barnaby replied. "In fact, I think you should shoot them."

"Just say the word, sir," said one of the four troopers.

"No, that won't be necessary," Wilkins said. "We

will leave them here to enjoy what little time they have left before the volcanoes erupt."

"Volcanoes?" Big Tom said. "There's going to be volcanoes?"

"Oh yes," Wilkins said. "The final stage of planetary upheavals before the portals close and the epoch ends."

"So the world will end with volcanoes," Big Tom said. "My science fair project was right. Sort of."

"You might survive the ash and lava long enough to see the demons arrive," Wilkins went on, "but I doubt it."

"What makes you think you'll escape?" Vincent said. "You really think Edwards is going to let you through the Portal?"

Mr. Wilkins's smile faltered, ever so slightly.

"Of course he will!" Barnaby said, crossing his fingers and waving them in Vincent's face. "Him and my dad are like this."

"We'll see," Vincent said, and just then there was a tap on his shoulder. "Now, how about you hand over those helicopters and surrender?"

Mr. Wilkins blinked in surprise.

"Say what?" Barnaby said.

"Are you trying to be funny?" Wilkins added.

"No," Vincent replied. "Optar?"

The wise old elf stepped forward, holding an Alphega communicator in his hands.

"Attention all pilots," he said into the comm. "You are now under my power. Land at once, or there will be pain."

The helicopters swerved in the air as the pilots attempted to disobey. Moments later they saw sense, and the choppers came down as ordered.

"What is going on?" Wilkins stammered, watching in disbelief.

"My cloaked friend Nod put obyons into your pilots' noses," Vincent said, "then took a communicator from one of your troopers."

All four troopers checked their belts, and one looked up sheepishly.

"Those helicopters," Optar added, "are now under our control."

"Huh?" said a suddenly very worried Barnaby.

"Interesting ploy," Wilkins said, "but useless. Troopers, kill them."

The four troopers took aim, but when they pulled their triggers nothing happened.

"I also asked Nod to safety all of your guns," Vincent said.

Clara, Nod, and Miss Sloam took that as their cue to act. They sprang forward into the troopers, fists flying. Mr. Wilkins and Barnaby watched in horror as their troops fell, then turned and viewed Vincent and his friends. There was fear in their eyes, and Vincent couldn't help but love it.

"Now," he said to them, "how about that ride?"

• • •

The three helicopters approached the Alphega Corporate Headquarters, leaving the ruined city behind them. The first helicopter carried Chanteuse and her mother, and Barnaby and his father. Optar had suggested leaving the Wilkinses behind, but Chanteuse wouldn't allow any lives to be lost.

The second carried the elves and the four captive troopers. The third carried Vincent, Max, their parents, Big Tom, and the two pixies.

The huge building had sustained no damage from either the earthquake or the tornadoes; it seemed the Portal Sites were the only safe places on Earth.

The trip took fifteen minutes, during which time Vincent and his brother tried to make their parents understand the situation. Mrs. Drear seemed to be taking it in, but Mr. Drear would not.

"You are all deceived," their father said for the tenth time. "Demons walk the Earth, and clearly the time of Tribulation has started, but there is nothing in the Text of the Triumvirate about Portal Sites!"

"But father," said Max, "perhaps these Portal Sites are what the Text was referring to when it said the Faithful would be taken from the world."

"The Text also says there will be doctrines of demons and false prophets, leading many astray," Mr. Drear shot back. "Are we to believe the word of these demons..."

"Pixies," Clara corrected.

"Silence!" Mr. Drear said to her, holding up his copy of the Text. "You have protected my sons, and for that I am grateful, but you are not spoken of in this Book, and so I cannot trust you."

"Sir," Nod said, "I met the guy who wrote that book."

"It was written by Jesus, Moses, and Abraham!" Mr. Drear shouted. "And they were inspired by God."

"It was written fifty years ago by an elf," Nod said, "who planted it into an archaeological site in Jerusalem. As a gag."

"Heresy!"

"Truth."

"Oh brother," said the pilot.

"Stay out of this," Vincent said, smacking the back of his helmet. "Look, Dad, if we show you the portal, will you at least consider it then?"

"No," his father replied. "And not one member of this family is going through that portal, either. As soon as we have vanquished the demons, we are going to build picket signs to keep people away from this place!"

"Oh boy," said the pilot.

"I told you, stay out of this," Vincent said, whacking his helmet again.

"Not you," the pilot said irritably. "Look at the other helicopters. They're under attack."

"Under attack?" Vincent said. "By what? Who's attacking them?"

"They're being swarmed," the pilot replied, "by demons."

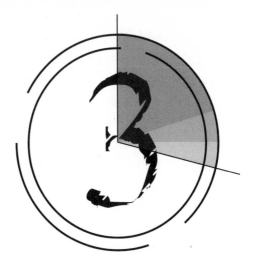

Vincent, Big Tom, and the others stared out the helicopter windows as they arrived in Alphega's airspace. It was true; one of the other helicopters was under attack from the demons, and the other one had already fallen. It lay in a burning wreck on the ground, with demons picking through it like vultures.

"No..." Vincent said. Friends of his had been in that helicopter.

The other helicopter swerved to avoid the demons, who fired themselves like missiles at its hold. Under such an attack, there was no way they could land safely. In fact, it seemed as if their fiery destruction was a certainty.

"What're they doing?" Big Tom asked. "I thought the demons were on their side."

"It's a feeding frenzy," Clara answered him. "They must have learned that post-epochal creatures were on board. And with the turning of the epoch so close at hand, they must be in a hunger craze."

There was a loud bang just then, followed by another and another. The helicopter had taken to shooting missiles at the demons, but the missiles had missed and hit the building instead.

"Oh, that's not good," the pilot said.

"Time to deal with the demon problem," Nod said, stripping off his apron pocket.

"Don't do that!" Vincent said. "The demons'll be able to taste you."

"Exactly," Nod said. "Some of them will come for me instead of the other chopper, and I'll be ready for them. You coming, Clara?" he added, picking up a spray can. The can was bigger than he was; he had to wrap one arm around it and press it to his chest, then reach up for the nozzle with his other hand.

"I'm right behind you," she said, taking another can. "Let us out!"

Vincent opened the side door, and the two pixies flew out and away. And good thing, too. Some of the demons were zooming in on them, no doubt reacting to Nod's presence. The pixies intercepted them, spraying hard and then speeding away to avoid the deadly mouths.

Their first attack had little effect. They were still too close to the helicopter, and the rotor blades interfered with the spray. One demon got some on his legs, and another on his chin, but not enough to do any serious harm. Nod and Clara led them away from the chopper, then spun around and sprayed at their pursuers. This time, the spray reached its mark, and four demons dropped from the sky.

So did the other chopper. As Vincent and Big Tom watched helplessly, the smoking helicopter plummeted straight toward the already-damaged building. Employees who had been evacuating ran screaming in all directions to avoid the coming crash.

At the last second, Miss Sloam leapt out the side

of the chopper, carrying Chanteuse, Barnaby, and Mr. Wilkins in her arms. She landed on her powerful legs and ran, while above her the helicopter crashed and exploded.

"Oh, no," Mrs. Drear gasped. "All those people..."

In a great rumble and a pluming cloud of dust, the northern half of the Alphega Corporate Headquarters collapsed. It was a terrible, terrifying sight, yet even through the dust cloud Vincent could see a ray of hope.

"The portal!" he cried, pointing at the bright glow shining through the ashen fog.

"Wow," said Big Tom.

"It's beautiful," said Mrs. Drear. "Gerald, can you see it?"

"I see it," Mr. Drear said. "It is a portal all right...to Hell!"

"Oh brother," said the pilot.

"Shut up," Vincent said, smacking his helmet again. "Take us down. We can't help our friends from up here."

"Are you kidding?" said the pilot. "I'm not going down there! It's dangerous."

Vincent wondered why the pilot was able to disobey, since he still had an obyon up his nose. Then he remembered the obyons only responded to elves, and there were none on board.

"You'll do as my brother tells you," Max said, rapping the pilot's helmet with his knuckles.

"No I won't," the pilot replied. "And stop hitting me. We could crash."

"We'll crash anyway when those demons get to us," Vincent pointed out. "On the ground you'll have a fighting chance."

"Good point," the pilot said. "Down it is."

The helicopter touched down without incident. The demons, it seemed, were busy elsewhere. Vincent noticed there seemed to be only two groups of them now, each chasing something.

"They're after the pixies!" Big Tom said as they jumped out of the helicopter.

"They must have finished with the elves," Vincent said sadly. Then he had a horrible thought. He looked around frantically, then relaxed when he saw Chanteuse and her mother not far away. The demons obviously hadn't realized the truth about Miss Sloam.

"Come on," Vincent said, grabbing two spray cans. "Let's help Nod and Clara."

Vincent ran toward the ruined building, waving his arms in the air. Big Tom ran after him, not knowing what Vincent was up to but copying his actions anyway.

"Why are we doing this?" Big Tom asked Vincent as he caught up.

"To get the pixies' attention," Vincent replied. "We want them to fly over us."

"Oh," Big Tom said. "Why?"

"I'll show you," Vincent said, because at that moment Clara was zooming down toward them with six demons in hot pursuit.

"Stand ready," Vincent said, readying his two cans.

"Oh, I get it!" Big Tom said, raising his own cans. "We're a trap!"

"Here they come," Vincent said as Clara flew past them. "Fire!"

Vincent and Big Tom let fly with their deadly, ozone-depleting mist as the demons flew in. Two took it full in the mouth, two got it on their arms and wings, and one noticed in time and flew up and over the spray. The last one ducked under the spray, ramming Vincent square in the chest.

The last thing Vincent thought before he blacked out was, "Not again…"

• • •

Vincent stood in a vat of glue, trying to make it to a racetrack finishline suspended across the far end. He struggled and heaved and pulled at his legs, but he was held fast.

"Okay, do I need to spell this one out for you?"

Vincent looked around and saw a familiar elf hovering over the glue beside him.

"Grimbowl!" he cried. "You're alive!"

"Nope," Grimbowl said sadly. "I'm afraid I'm taking the ultimate out-of-body experience, kid. The demons finally got me, just like they got the rest of us."

"No," Vincent said. "All the elves…Grimbowl, I'm so sorry."

"Wasn't so bad," Grimbowl said, taking Vincent's hand. "The others have gone on to the great tree village in the sky, but I stuck around on the off chance someone got knocked unconscious. Might have guessed it'd be you."

"Hey!"

"Time's short, kid," Grimbowl went on, tugging on Vincent's hand. "Let's get out of this dream so I can show you how to save the world."

Vincent had trouble accepting that his friend before him was dead. He clung tightly to the elf's astral hand, afraid that if he let go Grimbowl would vanish forever.

"Wipe that look off your face," Grimbowl said, yanking him out of the dream. "Strong emotions will pull you back to your body, remember? And I need you out here."

"I know," Vincent said as they hovered over his sleeping body, which Big Tom was trying to wake up. "It's just..."

"Mourn me later," Grimbowl said. "You know those magical wards keeping everyone on Earth from sensing the Portal Sites? Rennik told us how to disable them."

"How?" Vincent asked.

"Wards that powerful can only be created by a huge source of magic," Grimbowl said. "There were creatures in my day that could have done it by themselves, but who knows how they're doing it now..."

"Doing what?" Vincent prodded him.

"You have to destroy the power source," Grimbowl said. "But that isn't enough. First, you have to fly your astral form through the power source and touch the portal. When you destroy the power source, the spell will be reversed and the Calling will shoot out stronger than ever. Got it?"

"Fly through the power source, touch the portal, then blow the source up," Vincent said. "Got it. Hey! You're in astral form. Why can't..."

"I don't have a silver cord any more," Grimbowl explained. "My body's gone, remember? Your silver cord is what'll connect the portal to the power source. Sorry, should have explained that earlier."

"Okay, fine," Vincent said.

"One more thing," Grimbowl said, and he hovered right next to Vincent's astral form and whispered.

"You did what?" Vincent said.

"Tell her later," Grimbowl said. "And tell her I said sorry."

"Okay," Vincent said. "I'm ready."

"Good," Grimbowl said. "Now, all you've got to do is stay in astral form until you find the power source. It's got to be around here somewhere…"

"Uh oh," Vincent said.

Chanteuse and her mother were walking toward his body, accompanied by Barnaby and his father. Walking up behind them were none other than Mr. Edwards and his two robotic bodyguards, and they did not look happy.

"Francis Wilkins!" Mr. Edwards barked. "I understand you employed three company helicopters without my permission, and brought a multitude of persons here against my express instructions. Explain yourself."

"I went to rescue my son," Wilkins told his boss. "He was in danger."

"I see," said Edwards. "And these people?"

"They kidnapped us!" Barnaby cried, pointing at Miss Sloam. "She's a troll, you know."

"Barnaby!" Chanteuse cried.

"Oh, not good," Vincent said.

"Is she?" Edwards said.

"She sure is," Barnaby said, "and she's plotting to bring down the magic wards!"

Vincent felt rage boiling in him. Barnaby had betrayed them—again—in spite of everything they'd done for him.

"Calm down, kid," Grimbowl told him. "We still need to find that power source."

"I see," Edwards said, returning his attention to Mr. Wilkins. "You and your son not only brought post-epochal beings here, but you brought the very people who threaten me the most." As he spoke, he turned and looked over at Vincent's body. "Tell me, Francis, is there any reason I shouldn't simply leave you two behind with the rest of your species?"

Barnaby and his father's faces became masks of terror, but Vincent's astral face lit up with a sudden revelation. Mr. Edwards always talked about humans as if he were not one of them. That meant he was probably something else. Max's comments about the *Prisons & Poltergeists* book came back to him, and Vincent suddenly knew what something else was.

"I've found the power source," he told Grimbowl.

"Great," the elf's spirit answered. "Where?"

Before Vincent could answer, he saw Edwards nod to his bodyguards. The robots responded, raising their gauntlets and aiming them at Barnaby and his father.

"Then again, you have been useful to me in the past," Edwards went on, "and so I shall grant you both a far more merciful death."

Barnaby and his father turned to run, but they were too late. Horrified, Vincent looked away, but what he saw was just as chilling. The demons, led by Bix, were coming for Miss Sloam.

"They're going to kill Chanteuse's mother!" Vincent cried, frozen with cold dread.

"Vincent, control it!" Grimbowl said. "You have to..."

But it was too late. Vincent's soul snapped back to his body, and he woke up moaning in pain.

"Oh no," he cried, clutching at his chest. "Now what do we do?"

Vincent watched, helplessly, as the demons zoomed in around Miss Sloam. He tried to get up but couldn't, the pain in his chest was too great. Big Tom couldn't help him—he'd run straight into the battle, cans spraying. Vincent had never been so proud of his friend.

It was not enough, though. Big Tom's efforts were

keeping the demons at bay, but the cans would not last forever. Even if Vincent joined in with his own two cans, they still probably wouldn't kill them all. And if only one demon remained, Miss Sloam and the two pixies were dead.

Vincent had one advantage, though—he knew what the power source was. However, he couldn't project his soul out of his body to do what had to be done.

But there was one person left who could.

"Vincent, are you all right?"

Vincent raised his head and saw his brother running toward him. Their parents were right behind, carrying a couple of picket signs they'd managed to cobble together from items they'd found in the helicopter.

"Help me up," he wheezed, and Max took his arms and pulled him to his feet.

"Come along, boys," Mr. Drear said, dropping to his knees. "We will pray for strength, then we shall go forth and put an end to this portal heresy."

"Max," Vincent said, taking his brother's arm before he could kneel. "I need you to help Big Tom. And I need Chanteuse. She's the only one who can save the world."

"What?" said Max.

"What?" said Mr. Drear, rising to his feet in a split second. "The witch? No! That is the path of Evil!"

"I need her," Vincent told Max, squeezing his brother's arm hard. "Please. Everything depends on her."

"No!" Mr. Drear said, taking Max's other arm. "I forbid it! The Triumvirate forbids it!"

Max looked from his father to his brother. Vincent released his arm, lowered himself with his legs, and picked up the two remaining spray cans. He winced as he stood back up, but he didn't let the pain stop him.

"Please," he said, holding out the cans.

"Father," Max said, "there is more to the world than is written in any one book. I know what is right. Please release me."

Mr. Drear looked horrified beyond words, no doubt contemplating the loss of both his sons' souls to the lure of the occult. Vincent understood this, and knew they didn't have time for it. He raised a spray can and shot his dad right in the face.

"Gaagh!" Mr. Drear cried, releasing Max at once and covering his eyes.

"Vincent!" said Max. "Honor thy father and mother!"

"I'll honor them later," Vincent said, handing him the cans. "Go. Now."

Max rushed off toward the battle, where six demons swarmed around a scratched and bruised Miss Sloam. The two pixies had joined the fight, doing what they could and then dashing behind Big Tom for cover. And watching it all was Mr. Edwards, who seemed to be enjoying the fracas a great deal.

"You have betrayed the Triumvirate this day," Mr. Drear said, his eyes painfully bloodshot. "And you have damned your brother. On this, the Day of Judgment!" He raised his hand and swung at Vincent's face, but Mrs. Drear caught his wrist.

"Gerald, no," she said. "You know the Triumvirate works in mysterious ways. Perhaps this is the way of things. Perhaps our boys are right."

"You betray me as well?" Mr. Drear said. "Then I have no family. I have no sons, no wife. But I still have the Triumvirate." He pulled his hand roughly free from Mrs. Drear's, then he turned and stormed off.

"Dad, please stay," Vincent called after him. In the distance, he saw lava shooting into the sky from newly formed volcanoes, and his father was walking toward them.

"Let him go," his mother said, wiping away a tear.

"The Triumvirate gave all of us Free Will. He has made his choice, as have we, and we must respect it."

Vincent would have agreed, but he was distracted by the shouts coming from behind. He turned and saw Max dragging a very angry Chanteuse toward them.

"Let me go!" she said. "I will not abandon my mother!"

Vincent looked over their shoulders and saw Miss Sloam fighting with Max's spray cans. The number of demons had been cut down to five, and two of them looked very sick.

"My brother says you are needed," Max said. "You must come!"

"Chanteuse," Vincent said, walking toward her. "You must help us. Only you can do it."

"Do what?" she snapped, still struggling in Max's grip.

"Astral projection," Vincent said, and he told her briskly what he needed her to do. Chanteuse listened, then immediately refused.

"Vincent, I told you," she said. "I can't do that. Someone I care about will die."

"No, that won't happen," Vincent said. "The being

you saw? That was Grimbowl. He told me. He told you not to project because he didn't want you to know about the seedier things the elves have been up to."

"Grimbowl did that?" Chanteuse said. "That filthy little bugger!"

"He said he's very sorry," Vincent went on, "and hoped you'd find it in your heart to forgive him."

"I…well, that will come later," Chanteuse said, lying down. "Very well, Vincent. I will do as you have asked."

"Thank you," Vincent said. "Mom, please watch over her and keep her safe. Max, help me walk over to Mr. Edwards. I have something to say to him."

It took them a minute to walk over to the battle-ground. In that time another demon fell, and the remaining four looked pretty sick. They were more cautious now, hovering just out of spray range and looking for an opening to strike. Bix was one of them, for which Vincent was glad. Having a demon around that he knew by name would be handy.

"Mr. Edwards!" he called, and the half-man and his robot minders turned to look at him. "Mr. Edwards, I want to talk to you."

"What do you want?" Edwards said. His bodyguards had raised their gauntlets, and he did not discourage them.

"I just wanted to know how you feel," Vincent asked, "about us spraying aerosol into the air. You know, one last chance for us humans to pollute before the end."

"Indeed," Mr. Edwards said. "You humans do nay deserve the wonderful world you've been given."

"Humans are filthy, aren't they?" Vincent said.

"You certainly are!"

"Just like you," Vincent said.

"I most certainly am not!" Mr. Edwards roared. "My race has always been the cleanest..." He stopped, realizing what he'd said.

"Huh?" said Bix, turning to listen.

"That's right, Bix," Vincent said, sending it home. "He's a centaur. Aren't you, Mr. Edwards?"

"I...I am nay!" Mr. Edwards said, his mechanical legs taking a step back. His guards immediately took positions in front of him, and re-targeted their gauntlets at Bix.

"You may have lost your horse-half," Vincent said, "but that doesn't change what you are. You're the only creature with enough magical energy to power the wards."

"You know," said Bix, drifting closer, "there was a story about a centaur who got away."

"Yeah," said another demon, joining Bix. "His whole lower half was bitten off, but he escaped into a cave or something."

"Stop them!" Mr. Edwards cried. "Keep them away from me."

The bodyguards fired their electrical bolts, stunning the demons but not stopping them. Bix dropped under their defense and bit clean through a bodyguard's chest. It collapsed to the ground, sparks flying from the wound. The second bodyguard fell just as quickly, though in much smaller pieces.

"Get back, all of you," Mr. Edwards said. He waved his hand at Vincent and Max, and a force like the wind knocked them both over. "Stay away! Or I'll...ulg!"

Vincent guessed, correctly, that the spirit of Chanteuse had just passed through him. Perfect timing, if ever there had been. The demons took full advantage of Mr. Edwards's distraction and zoomed in, and moments later the only thing remaining of Alphega Corp.'s founder was his mechanical legs.

"Yikes," said Vincent. "That was..."

And then he couldn't speak. He and everyone else on the planet felt a powerful compulsion, a near-overwhelming desire to get to a portal site. Vincent felt the pull coming directly from the portal, and would have known it was there without looking, without even knowing what it was.

"We did it," he said, turning to Max. "We...no!"

The four remaining demons had turned, and stared hungrily at Miss Sloam and the pixies. Nod, Clara, and Miss Sloam hadn't seen them, nor had Big Tom, so wrapped up were they in the portal's call. And there was a rolling sound...

Vincent looked down. Big Tom's spray cans had fallen from his limp fingers, and they rolled toward him.

Vincent ran, grabbing Max's hand and pulling him along. The demons charged, their mouths open. Vincent ignored his pain and scooped the cans up, snapping off the nozzles as he did so. Spray poured out of the tops of the cans as Vincent gave one to Max and tossed the other. Max got the idea and tossed his own.

The first one hit Miss Sloam in the shoulder. The second hit her head. She turned, and saw the demons almost upon her. However, the spray in the air made the demons stop and gag. Miss Sloam raised both her cans and emptied them into the demons' mouths.

"Close," said Max, watching as the demons shriveled and melted on the ground.

"Too close," Vincent agreed. "Well, shall we go? The world's about to end."

The whole world over, people got the message. Human and post-epochal creatures alike dropped what they were doing and journeyed to the nearest portal site. Some were lucky enough to be close by; their trek was short. Others had a longer way to go, and their chances of making it in time were slim.

That any of them had a chance at all was a miracle. The actions of a few brave humans, two pixies, nine elves, and one troll had made all the difference.

Four of those humans, one of the pixies, and the troll sat by the edge of the portal, watching as people arrived by the dozens. Vincent absently watched them stream in, his mind lost in thought.

"What do you figure the next race will be?" Vincent asked Chanteuse, who sat next to him beside her mother. "Cockroaches? Or dolphins, maybe?"

"My money's on dolphins," Nod said, slouching on Miss Sloam's shoulder. "Big brains. I bet the second we go, one of them'll evolve opposable thumbs."

"I say roaches," Miss Sloam said. "They know how to survive anything."

"That's what Big Tom would have said," Vincent told them.

Big Tom had already passed through the portal. Half an hour earlier he'd been reunited with his parents. It seemed they'd been having car trouble when the earthquake struck, and hadn't been able to get home. Vincent had smiled widely as Big Tom filled them in on what had happened, and how their spray cans had saved them all.

"It might be a creature we know nothing about," Chanteuse suggested. "Who knows what Mother Earth will create?"

They pondered that in silence for a few minutes.

"I'm with Nod," Vincent decided. "Dolphins."

"We should go," Max said. "We probably don't have much time left."

"Just give Clara a few more minutes," Vincent said.

"Don't worry," Nod added. "She never fails."

As if summoned by her name, Clara appeared above the heads of the crowd. Vincent couldn't see her right away, but he could clearly see the one she carried.

"Put me down!" shouted Vincent's father, flailing his arms and legs helplessly. "In the name of the Triumvirate, I command you to release me this instant!"

"He wasn't hard to find," Clara said. "He was the only one walking in the wrong direction."

"I thought we'd agreed he'd made his choice," said Vincent's mother, though she sounded more relieved than critical.

"He did," Vincent replied, holding out his arm for his brother to help him up. "And I made mine. Just this once, let me force my beliefs on him?"

Mr. Drear kept arguing and thrashing as Clara carried him into the portal. Chanteuse and her mom stood up and went next, followed by Mrs. Drear.

"Here we go," Vincent said. The parts of his chest that were not in pain swelled with excitement. Then, feeling that something should be said to mark the historic occasion, he turned and looked back at the planet he'd called home.

"Thanks," he said. "It's been fun."

Then he and Max stepped through the portal into the mystery beyond.

• • •

Two hours later, the portal sites closed. Those who hadn't made it felt a strong sense of loss.

A few minutes after that, some new portals opened in the sky. Out of those portals, demons poured by the thousands. People ran. Some tried to hide. But all of them knew one thing for certain.

Their time was up. This was, well and truly...

The End of the World.

About the Author

Timothy Carter was born in England during the week of the last lunar mission, and he turned thirteen on Friday the 13th. He grew up in Canada's National Capital Region, and studied drama at Algonquin College.

His first YA novel, *Attack of the Intergalactic Soul Hunters*, was published in 2005. Timothy lives, writes, and watches for signs of the apocalypse in Toronto with his wife and cat.